# Praise for *Blue Runaways*

"Iceland, Vietnam, Bali, Italy—Jann Everard's vividly drawn characters may travel far from home, but cannot avoid a reckoning with the fundamentals of life, including death. *Blue Runaways* is a thought-provoking and bittersweet collection, well worth the read."

*—Kathy Page, author of the Giller-nominated* Paradise and Elsewhere *and* Dear Evelyn, *winner of the Rogers Writers' Trust Fiction Prize*

"Each of the stories in *Blue Runaways* is a gorgeous slice of time and place, filled with characters who struggle with connection and disconnection, passion and compassion, love and its absence. Jann Everard writes with an eye for detail and with lots of heart. Her bang-on observations, delivered with empathy, make these stories a delight."

*—Lori Hahnel, author of* Vermin: Stories *and* Flicker

"Jann's stories travel the world: from Iceland to Bali; from the grasslands of the Canadian prairies to Italy; and more. As skilled as she is at evoking these disparate places, she is equally skilled at travelling the inner human landscape. I have ridden right along with Jann's heroines as they grapple with life's big questions and emotions, and have come away feeling enriched. I loved these stories."

*—Lynn Thomson, author of* Birding with Yeats

"With compassion and sparkling wit, these stories deftly explore the unexpected confluence of loss and desire. Everard has a painter's eye for landscapes—both foreign and familiar—and a storyteller's skill in communicating how the natural world shapes our humanity. Read them slowly, and savour them."

*—Carleigh Baker, author of* Bad Endings *and finalist for the Rogers Writers' Trust Fiction Prize*

"*Blue Runaways* is very outdoorsy, with characters in canoes and snowshoes, spelunking in Iceland and touring Bali, but Everard also communes with wine and divorce, human loss and mysterious adaptations, sketching vibrant scenes and scapes with amazing empathy. Blue Runaways is meditative, cathartic, and brimming with life; it sings."

*—Mark Anthony Jarman, author of* Burn Man: Selected Stories *and the travel book* Touch Anywhere to Begin

"I had the pleasure of working with Jann Everard on early versions of these stories and was impressed from the start by her confidence, her curiosity, her compassion, and her keen insight into the secrets we keep even from ourselves. The women in these pages are indeed "blue runaways," trying to escape the uncomfortable truth that they—and those they love—are mortal, and that it is impossible for people to protect each other. Exploring how they come to this realization and how they respond to it, Everard is at once unsparing and deeply kind.

"But in addition to the 'blue' element that human life swims in, there is another world: the natural world in which people seek, and sometimes find, refuge. Reading these stories is a wide-eyed visit not just to the icy challenge of winter camping in Ontario and the dry heat of summer camping in Saskatchewan but also to an Italian garden, a Bali redolent of rambutans and jasmine, and an Icelandic cave full of phosphorescent algae. Everard maps the non-human world as expertly as she does the mind's divagations and the body's appetites."

*—Susan Glickman, author of* Cathedral/Grove *and sixteen other books of poetry and prose*

# BLUE RUNAWAYS

# BLUE RUNAWAYS

STORIES

JANN EVERARD

ISBN: 978-1-73899330-7
eBook ISBN: 978-1-73899331-4

1 2 3 4 5 6 7 8 9 10

The following stories were previously published in different form: "Blue Runaways" in *The Malahat Review*; "Through the Sidelights" and "Watching Her Breath" in *The New Quarterly*; "An Imitation of Grace" in *Grain*; "Lost Language" in *EVENT*; "Memento Mori" in *Humber Literary Review*; "Force Field" and "Relative Grief" in *Room Magazine*; "The Bus Stops Here" in *The Fiddlehead*; "Beyond Cure" in *Grain* as "No Pain in Nature"; and "Housing Crisis" in *Agnes and True*.

Cataloguing Data available from Library and Archives Canada.

Author photograph by Milena Paige Creative
Interior designed by Ned Seager

Printed and bound in Canada by Friesens

Stonehewer Books | Victoria, BC
stonehewerbooks.com

Stonehewer Books is located on the traditional territory of the Lkwungen people on what is now called Vancouver Island. We acknowledge and are grateful for the unique contributions to our common well-being made by the Indigenous peoples of this land.

*For Jim*

# Contents

# Blue Runaways

At the Keflavík International Airport, Liv held up a cardboard sign that read Artists, and I eyed her for twenty minutes before realizing it meant me. In red pants, red boots, red sweater, red lipstick, she looked like she'd been turned inside out, a beating heart exposed. As we waited for a painter from France, she poured me brutish coffee from a thermos and said, "So, are you here to make art, or are you here to escape?"

I gestured at my empty left sleeve. "I'm depressed."

"You only need one hand to give the finger," she said. "Have a *kleinur*." She took back my coffee cup and handed me a twisted donut. The gummy dough stuck to my teeth.

"How old are you?" she asked.

"Twenty-four."

"You still live at home?"

"My parents needed a break from me. They're paying for this."

Liv surveyed my body from top to bottom. A flush ignited at my neck, fired up my cheeks. With little more than a glance I felt she understood me, every shade of pain and anger and loneliness I'd felt since my surgery. "Like sending you away to summer camp," she said. "Do you think your folks are making out right now—a little afternoon delight? Or do you have siblings who'll spoil the mood?"

"I'm an only child."

She tapped the left side of her chest. I couldn't tell if she was trying to suggest shared experience or pity.

"Some old psychologist called that a disease in itself." She held my gaze too long to be comfortable. "Every day, hundreds of visitors arrive here seeking the same thing. But you'll see soon enough. This island breeds loneliness. It wasn't made for artists or for sun-filled romance."

I'm not an artist of any kind. I'm a lost soul, a person searching for a purpose in life—according to my mom. "You just feel like you're in a hole right now," she said to me a month ago, the euphemism as close to truth as her maternal instincts would allow. She means well, so I haven't told her it's worse than that. I'm looking for a purpose to live.

She handed me tickets to an Icelandic arts retreat. "You know what I've always told you to do when you find yourself in a hole." I nodded reflexively as Mom sat on my good side, flipping the pages of tourism brochures. Images of waterfalls, fluffy baby puffins, and the pink shoulders of men and women lounging in thermal baths filled the pages. I think she secretly hoped I'd meet someone in Iceland who would care for me better than she could. Parents are always looking for fairy tale endings for their children.

LIV DROVE THE PAINTER and me from the airport to the guest-house. It took four hours by Jeep in a slanting rain the sun never managed to thrust aside. "This is the famous Ring Road," Liv said, after glancing back to make sure the painter was asleep. "You can drive around the whole damn island in a week. Every gas station serves the same hot dogs and pastries. You'll only see lava, the ocean, and moss. Unless it stops raining; then, you might see a glacier. After a while you'll realize there are more horses here than people can possibly ride." She made chewing motions and waited for me to look horrified. As she shoved a CD into the dust-covered dash, I noticed the case was familiar. "Wild Horses" blasted from the speakers, but the painter in the back didn't wake up, even when Liv sang the chorus off-key.

"Did you bring good weather with you?" she demanded when the song ended. "I could use some fucking sun."

She made a sudden right turn onto a side road without signalling, throwing me against her so that my surgical stump bumped up against her shoulder. She pulled onto the verge and baaed out the window at three ewes standing motionless nearby. "There's nothing here you can't get where you live except volcanoes that erupt without warning. Most of the island is bleak and treeless." She turned to me with damp lashes and down-turned lips, the shiny red lacquer chewed away. "I don't get it. Iceland is small and remote and wet. Why do you people keep coming here? What do you all hope to find?"

THE GUESTHOUSE IS IN the middle of nowhere. The next farm is thirty minutes away, the next town an hour. Although my parents paid for me to have a private room, a broken pipe has made it uninhabitable. Liv says, "She'll sleep with me," and the eyes of every other participant narrow with jealousy or suspicion. They've been on site a week already and have staked their claims to her attention with earnest sketches and eco-friendly collages. I soon understand that Liv is considered communal property. When she enters a room, everyone shouts "Liv!" like she's a long-lost relative or that dude Norm on reruns of *Cheers*. She is the *dóttir* of the house, the arts instructor, the centre of a small universe. Next to Liv, the painter and I are just two more gulls in the cloud-sodden air, two more grey chunks of basalt on the fields that surround us.

In the morning workshop, Liv invites us to draw icebergs. We are only allowed to use blue crayons. Liv has amassed an impressive range of blues, each wax stick stripped of its protective paper. "The bergs hive off the glaciers and float away to sea," Liv says, as she fills a page of her sketchbook with extraordinary shapes, hidden faces straining seaward from within each one. "Blue runaways," she says in a voice that sounds so wistful everyone at the table looks up. She sharpens a crayon and her conciliatory smile is as unnatural as the turquoise she holds. "Imagine elsewhere," she says. "Think warm, seaside carnival. Think cotton candy and Blue Cherry Gatorade."

Liv disappears after the Tuesday afternoon workshop. Since it is karaoke night, the guesthouse bustles with communal dinner preparations. Four artists from Denmark hover over a slab of fish that glistens on brown paper wrapping, sharing festive recipes. Two German girls giggle as they peel a mound of potatoes with the dexterity of seasoned kitchen help. I try to catch the eyes of the twin brothers from the States, but they are juggling the pallid tomatoes and cucumber they will douse with oil and call a salad. The Frenchman pops the cork on a bottle of wine. Invisibility is what I have come to expect since I became one-armed, so I retire to a corner to arrange crackers on a plate. I cut wedges of Jarlsberg with my right hand by draping the brick of cheese with a tea towel and anchoring it with my stump. My face must be very close to the cheese to accomplish this task, but I hold my breath so I don't contaminate the food. After dinner, the group sings. I wait in the kitchen, and Liv's voice soars over the others to reach me like a siren's song. On a shelf below the counter, I find the cheese tray, soggy crackers topped with wedges that are dry and curling. I rearrange the crackers to spell out LIV.

I WAKE UP to cutlery clattering. It's still dark but Liv is not in her bunk above me. When I find her in the kitchen, she has sliced half a dozen onions and piled them high in a cast iron frying pan. She stirs the twisted rings with a wooden spoon, tears streaming down her face.

"Are you okay?" I ask, and she shakes her head.

"Let me," I say, taking the spoon and bumping her away from the stove with my hip. I can do this for her: stir and stir the onions until they go translucent, sweeten, and caramelize. I sense they are an excuse for Liv to have a good cry. "Why don't you just leave, if you hate it here so much?" I say, and she asks me why I don't just snap out of it if I'm so depressed.

Then she sinks down to the floor, her back against the shelves.

The air is thick with vapours that sting the eyelids, and more people are drawn from their bedrooms to investigate the smell. They look at me with irritation before retreating, unaware that out of their lines of sight, Liv leans her head against my thigh, whispering, "Sorry, sorry." Once they're gone, I crouch beside her. We feed each other the glistening rings, twinned together by the odours that cling to our clothes, our hair, our oily breath. "What would it take?" I ask, knowing some reasons have to be big enough. Her eyes rest on my empty sleeve as she shakes her head. She sees the cheese tray before I can nudge the crackers back into disorder.

LIV IS WHITE-BLONDE with eyes the colour of reindeer moss. Her skin has the blue cast of fine porcelain, a scattering of freckles across the nose. She is long limbed with taut muscles and whorled ears studded with silver Celtic knots. A Nordic goddess, a snow queen. On my third morning at the guesthouse, I wake to find her standing naked close by my bunk. She has no pubic hair, just red stipple as if each strand has been waxed away or plucked.

"You make me think of old European paintings," I say.

She kneels by my bed and caresses my shoulder, then moves her thumb down to my stump. Her hair falls in front of her face like one of the waterfalls we passed on the way to the guesthouse. *Foss* means waterfall means oh my God, I *feel* her fingers on the missing limb. "How did you lose your arm?" she asks.

I open my mouth to tell her the story of my accident, and her lips graze my ear. "Not here," she says. In the silvery light of morning, she tosses clothes my way. "Get dressed."

"I'll be too hot in these," I say, too hot already.

"Not where we're going," she answers, and helps me pull one of her own woolly sweaters over my head. The struggle to clothe myself has, until now, been a private one, so this feels as intimate as if Liv's run her hands over my breasts. I sense some longing pent up in her, but I'm too inexperienced at this to know whether it's sexual, too stunned to believe it's directed at me.

"What about the others? The workshop?" I ask, wanting Liv to tell me that we are an island unto ourselves. She wipes her hands together as if brushing off dirt. "Let them paint landscapes," she says.

LIV DRIVES HARD through the curtain of rain, the Jeep spitting gravel. The hard hat she hands me slides forward so I can barely see. We park in a lava field and walk to a place where the rocky surface has collapsed into a chasm. She precedes me down a ladder and I can sense her hovering, ready to provide a steady hand if the wind blasts or I lose my hold. At the bottom, she grasps my fingers. "There's no path. It's hard to walk here and keep your balance."

To Liv, I must be transparent. I've told everyone—my surgeon, my social worker, my parents—that I feel unbalanced by my missing arm and by the driver of that other car who continues to hound me, trying to apologize for my loss. They all hear me, but they do not *hear* me. "Tap into your creativity!" my mother exclaims, as if I can imagine myself a new limb, draw myself as attractive, and this will fix everything.

We enter a cave. Where it narrows, there is a locked gate.

Liv opens it with an iron key and waves me in, turning on the headlamp attached to my helmet. Stumbling after her, I become aware of how quiet the place is. It absorbs our sound; there are no echoes. It's my first experience of Iceland without the pelting rain and howling wind. Once we've reached a large chamber, Liv stops and pats a flat boulder that will seat both of us. "This is where I come when I need to dream," she says. "Look up." She puts an arm around me, directing the beams of our headlamps to a phosphorescent glow on the upper cavern walls. "Fungi," she says, "that live here because they are adapted to this and only this environment, poor things."

She lets me take in their glow before continuing. "Have you ever been in a lava tube before? Way back in history, molten rock moved through here while the surface crusted over. The channel goes on forever—nearly sixteen hundred metres, apparently. All my life I've imagined it leads to the centre of the Earth, Jules Verne-like—to some other world. Until now, I've never had the nerve to explore it. I've been afraid there's no escape. It's considered crazy to want to leave Iceland, you know."

She reaches over to extinguish my headlamp, then turns off her own. We are in the deepest dark I have ever experienced. My brain wants to see some aura of Liv, but everything is black.

"Do you want to tell me what happened to you?" she asks.

My mother always said there are only two options when you find yourself in a hole: dig deeper—or reach for the hand that will pull you out. For a long time, I have been digging. "Yes," I say, and then I tell Liv about the cars skidding on ice. I tell her that one arm is enough to push away everyone you love, and that I can't see my life stretching out past twenty-four. "You could lock me in this tube and throw away the key," I say.

From nowhere, Liv's fingers quest on my cheek, turning my face toward hers. In the cold air of the cave, our warm breath pools between us.

"You don't mean that," she says and makes her pledge with a kiss. It feels huge, and I'm roused to some equal promise. I wrap my arms around her—feel whole as I do.

Liv leans her forehead against mine. "Tomorrow, I want you to lock me in here and let me walk into the dark."

The idea is ridiculous, yet perfect. She'll find her answer at the end of the tunnel, and no one will think her crazy. Of the many reasons to leave a place, this is one everyone agrees on.

She seeks out my hand, closing my fingers over the iron key. "And when I get back to the gate..." She doesn't ask at that moment. She doesn't need to ask me directly. I can read her, even in the dark. She wants to know that once she's hit rock bottom and looks back up, she can count on someone to be there. It's something I can promise. I only need one hand to reach down and pull her up. One hand to lead her away.

# Through the Sidelights

The lemon cost ninety-nine cents. Meg handed the cashier a dollar and waited half a second until the woman turned away. Of course there would be no change. Pennies no longer circulated. But she wanted one nonetheless. Mourned the penny's loss as she mourned so many things that had disappeared forever: the clacking of typewriters, the flavour of wild strawberries, the silence of Sunday mornings, and Rachel, her oldest friend.

The two months that had elapsed since Rachel's death felt more like two days. When Meg's thoughts turned to their last moments together, her breath hitched in her throat—sleep apnea without the sleep. David had said she'd been more emotional about the loss of Rachel than the loss of her own mother. He'd apologized immediately, put his arms around her as she wilted. "I shouldn't have said that," he'd whispered, but it was true. The death of her ninety-year-old mother had felt natural; the death of Rachel felt like an amputation.

Back in her kitchen, she sprinkled grated lemon zest on top of the pasta casserole, its fresh tang opening another door to memories. Vodka and lemonade in the yard. Lemon-scented nail polish remover at that spa on Adelaide. The swabs the hospital had supplied for Rachel's dry mouth.

The casserole dish fit snugly into its insulated bag. David spoke without waiting for her to face him. "How long are you going to keep doing this, Meg?"

She turned and stood very still before replying. "How long do you think Rachel would've kept feeding you if I'd died?"

He sighed. "It's not that I don't admire what you're doing. It's very kind of you. But it's not a measure of your friendship to keep taking her husband food. And he doesn't expect it. At some point, you're going to have to stop, and Joe is going to have to start cooking for himself."

"I know. Soon." She wiped a little sauce off the lid and zipped up the bag. "But it's only been, what, six weeks? And half the time Carly drops Joe's dinner off for me on her way to the library. She's been great, really. Is she still here?"

"It's been eight weeks, Meg. And Carly left two hours ago. Her grades this term aren't very good, you know. I'm worried about her." He poked at the remaining pasta in the pot with a wooden spoon. She'd been preparing more elaborate recipes every day. The steam wafted scents of cumin and sumac, a spice she'd never used before. She could see that David had more he wanted to say but was choosing not to. He'd always had a high degree of self-regulation. She waited, as she always waited, to see if his fuse would finally light. Part of her wished he'd choose the path to argument—a big roaring fight that would change something about their relationship.

"Say hi to Joe for me," he said instead. "Tell him I'll drop by in a few days." He kissed her cheek lightly. "Be careful driving home in the dark, love."

THIS TIME, she didn't walk in the front door like she usually did. She rang the doorbell instead.

"It was open," Joe told her when he answered, twisting the doorknob back and forth to check.

"I know. But it's time you had your privacy back." She waited until he waved her in, followed when he led the way to the kitchen.

She ignored the dirty plates teetering in the sink and the cluttered kitchen table. From the shelf where Rachel had always kept them, she removed two wineglasses and filled them from the open bottle of Baco Noir on the counter. A pile of magazines rested on her usual seat at the table. She added them to another. She would keep Joe company so he didn't have to eat alone. She'd usher in the evening with him, knowing how hard that part of the day could be.

He hovered near the table, then finally sat. "I'm befuddled," he said.

"Befuddled?" She raised her wineglass, gestured at him to open the thermal bag himself. "Catering continues for now, but maid service is over."

They'd known each other for more than thirty years. She and Rachel, David and Joe. Gone to school together, married the same year, bought houses in the same neighbourhood. The women had conspired to be on maternity leaves together, succeeded the first time. The men had played tennis on Sundays, sometimes with the kids, sometimes on their own. They'd shared cottages and confidences, celebrated birthdays and anniversaries. She'd never heard Joe use the word befuddled before, and it shocked her that he could still surprise.

She poured herself more wine.

Joe lifted out the casserole and reached for a fork. "The boys called today," he said. "They both got paid for their bereavement leave."

"They're lucky to have jobs with benefits. That's so rare now."

They'd talked about this often in Rachel's last bedridden days—how Rachel's two sons and Meg's Kyle had studied engineering at the right time, when jobs were plentiful. The three young men had flown home together for the funeral. Meg had paid for Kyle's ticket, wanting him and Carly near her. She'd been surrounded by sickness for so long.

"I started going through her things today." Joe spoke between bites, watching her twist her wedding ring.

"That's good."

"You want any of her clothes?"

"No, but thanks for asking."

"I need help with her jewellery and papers."

"Hold on to the jewellery for the boys. They'll get married some day and can give the pieces they like to their wives. Burn the papers."

Joe stared at her, deep brown eyes pleading.

"Okay, I'll do the papers for you," she said. "How's the pasta?"

"Excellent. You were always the better cook, you know. I never told Rach that, of course."

"Of course."

He chewed. She drank. It occurred to her that while she and Rachel had looked less like each other as they'd aged—Rachel bloating then thinning in the various stages of her illness, Meg thickening under stress—Joe and David looked more and more alike. Joe was tall, David broad across the shoulders, but both were now hunched, as if they carried invisible burdens. The skin on their faces had softened and puckered. Joe had missed a spot on his jawline when he shaved. David often did that too. They didn't look like old men, not yet. But they'd both become craggy.

"You've been looking at the old albums?" Meg pulled the brown binder across the table.

He nodded. "There are hardly any pictures of her. She was always the photographer."

Meg flipped the book open to the middle. Ottawa. In photo after photo, she stood between Joe and David, each with a stroller, first babies in tow. In her mind, she looked like a woman with two husbands. Or like either man could be her husband. No sign indicated she favoured one over the other—no slight lean or unconscious coordination of clothes.

Joe scraped his fork against the bottom of the empty dish, a chalk-on-board screech. "Sorry," he said, cringing at the noise. "I can't find the pictures of Paris."

"First trip or second?"

"First."

Meg remembered taking the photo he was looking for: Rachel, kneeling on the path next to the Seine, asking Joe to marry her. Rachel had planned the whole thing, thinking herself audacious to be the one who proposed. On the plane home, David had leaned over the armrest and asked Meg to marry him. She'd felt the moment tarnished—too close on the heels of their friends' engagement, too impromptu—but she'd still said yes.

The wine was a potent red, blood warm, full of tannins that coated her teeth. Already her cheeks had flushed a little. The tendons and veins of her hand, cupped around the bowl of the wineglass, popped high above the surface of her skin. Was that a new liver spot by her knuckle? What was making her so tense?

Joe stopped chewing, then stood up. "Come with me. I want to show you something."

The hall, hushed by carpet, was dimly lit. The house felt too silent as they passed the boys' childhood bedrooms and the spare room—all three doors closed. Joe walked into the master suite, but Meg stopped in the doorway, unwilling to pass through. She could count on one hand the number of times she'd been in this room—two post-delivery visits to Rachel, another when her friend had been flattened by flu. They'd shared so much, knew so many details of each other's lives, but they'd respected their bedrooms, agreeing as young, working mothers that it was the one place in the house where a closed door was just as likely to signal a hasty cleanup before visitors as a need for privacy.

She didn't recognize the navy duvet cover or the golden drapes and wondered if they were new. Rachel had not wanted to be sick or die in her marital bed, so she'd moved to the spare room's built-in as soon as she was diagnosed as palliative. Later, that bed had been replaced with a hospital loaner that could be raised and lowered electronically. "Joe and I'll be able to add a few more positions to our repertoire," Rachel had joked, pressing the buttons as she'd waited unsteadily for Meg to straighten the foam pad that cushioned her fragile skin.

"I'll get the box," Joe said, as Meg stared into the half-empty closet and then at the unmade bed. Joe had piled clothes there, including Rachel's brocade robe, royal blue with fake-fur trim and lining and a braided belt. It was both regal and gorgeous, a theatrical garment that flooded Meg with another wave of grief. She needed to get out of the room. Suddenly it smelled like the ocean, salty like recent sex.

"Hang on. I've got it." Joe dangled a strand of white pearls from their clasp. "Remember these?" The beads glistened in the bedroom's light. Rachel had worn them on her wedding day. Meg had worn a matching pink set. "I don't think she wore them again after the wedding," he said. "She didn't really like pearls, but she knew you did. You should keep these." He stretched out his hand. When she didn't take the necklace, he moved behind her to clasp it around her neck. Her hair got in the way and so she reached back to lift it. She closed her eyes and imagined herself anywhere but in this room. But Joe's touch, light and fluttery against her nape, was too much. He caught her as she began to crumple, arms reaching from behind, hands folding over the upper curves of her breasts. For what seemed like a long time, they stood in this odd embrace. Meg could hear Joe's breath. It felt deep and rhythmic compared to hers. She thought she felt his lips against her neck. What was happening felt both desperate and wrong, and yet she could not stop herself. She laid her own hands over Joe's, drawing his fingers down until they splayed over her nipples, hard and erect against her cotton t-shirt. She needed him to feel them. He didn't pull away.

"MOM, WHY ARE YOU SITTING in the dark?" Carly flipped on the kitchen light.

Meg squinted and covered her eyes with the palm of her hand, cooled by iced vodka.

"Hi, sweetheart. How was the library?" She moved to the sink, hoping Carly would think she'd been drinking water.

"Fine. I got there late. I dropped by to see Joe first. We're going to start playing tennis again soon. I thought maybe you'd seen me leave when you came by with his dinner again."

"No, I didn't see you, and Uncle Joe didn't mention it. But I'm sure he appreciated the company." She looked at her daughter closely, wondering if she'd caught an accusatory tone. Rachel's treatments had left her needing significant care, but she'd begged Meg to help her stay out of hospital, even when it was clear home care wasn't enough. Meg had considered herself blessed to have a daughter who seemed so mature and understanding about her mother's absences. But after all the time Meg had spent with Rachel in the last two years, Carly had every right to feel neglected.

"Dad said you're finding your courses a bit tough this term. Want to talk about it?" She sat down again, hoping to reclaim her role as mother.

Carly shook her head. "Aren't we past that? I'm going to finish this degree. Then get a job and move out."

The sense of rejection was immediate, even if it was misplaced. Meg hadn't thought Carly was in such a hurry to leave home. Before she could muster any response, her daughter was up and gone. She called out Carly's name, just as Joe had called out hers when they'd broken apart and she'd bolted for the door. Now she couldn't think of what to do. Whatever air had been in the room had been sucked out, leaving Meg feeling shrink-wrapped. This is what guilt feels like, she thought. Guilt for neglecting her daughter in favour of her friend, guilt for betraying David and Rachel today—people she loved deeply—and guilt for whatever she was feeling for Joe. At some level she knew the attraction was not real, that it was a common if not clichéd response to shared grief. Still, a niggling thought had taken root.

THE FLOORBOARDS CREAKED as Meg made her way toward the open door of her and David's bedroom. There was nothing in that room that could surprise her. It was familiar—the off-white walls, the off-white eiderdown. Why was their bedroom so colourless? Why no royal blues, no shining golds?

David snored gently, audible from the doorway. She veered back down the hall. No, the kitchen was too close to the booze. She needed cold air, to bundle up and sit on the back deck for a while. To freeze her thoughts, cool her fantasies.

The neighbour's motion-activated light flicked on, then off, as she pulled a patio chair out from under the table and brushed off a dusting of snow. A few stars burned through the city's dome of light. Tomorrow, the temperatures would soar; she could feel it in the warm wind already.

She knew middle age was messy, the subject of whispered conversations with friends in coffee shops and teary confessions over wine. Divorce was common, the result of empty nests and hormonal tsunamis. It was hard to think of romance at home in the face of greying pubic hair, night sweats, and conversations that stuck on repeat. And for several years now—since before Rachel's illness—Meg had felt as if she'd lost her sense of purpose, was merely notching up days that were safe and routine. If she were to die tomorrow, she wondered, would a reputation for reliability and loyalty be legacy enough? Would she feel as if she'd truly lived?

They had talked about all of this, she and Rachel, her friend becoming more and more arch and unfiltered as the treatments failed.

"What really sucks about dying at this age is that I'll never see the other side of menopause. The 'fuck you, I'm my own person' stage of life. Sometimes I get mad at Joe because I'm jealous. He has the chance to have another relationship, but I'll never feel first lust again, that delicious sensation when your cunt just wants to Hoover a guy."

"Rachel, Jesus!"

"Oh God, Meg, don't be a prude. All I have left are my might-have-beens. My death solves the middle-aged crisis for both Joe and me."

"Neither of you has ever been the crisis type. You're both too rock solid."

"But maybe we wouldn't have been forever. I told Joe he should find someone new right away. I told him that a year ago. If he's been smart, he'll have someone in the wings already. Maybe he has. I don't know. So, don't judge him if he follows my advice, okay? I sustain myself these days dreaming about lovers in my next life. Remember Harris from that third-year seminar we took? Remember Li Ping Chen? I always thought that behind those dollar store glasses hid someone who smouldered."

Meg had laughed, saying, "Stop, Rachel, you're killing me," then covered her mouth. "Poor Li Ping passed away, remember? An aneurysm."

"Well, maybe I can be his ghost bride then. In China, you know, some families marry the corpse of a dead woman to the corpse of a dead bachelor so the guy won't be lonely and haunt his family. I read that online. An afterlife party with sex. I like the idea of that." She'd started gasping for air then and had to rest a while. When she'd pulled herself back up on the pillow, she reached for Meg's hand, gaze intent, pupils dilated. "I worry about you. Your life seems profoundly sad and dull. You've stripped yourself of any identity except for mother and wife and caregiver to me. I love David, you know I do, but promise me that after all this, you'll do something—I don't know—something..." Her bottom lip cracked, marked by a bead of blood.

Rachel's observations stung, whether drug-induced or not. In the circumstances, Meg knew she had to rally. She leaned forward to blot the blood with a tissue. "Do you mean something audacious?"

Tears had sprung to both their eyes. "Oh, honey, haven't we been there, done that?" Rachel spluttered. "Up the ante. I think you should do something impetuous. Something downright rash!"

Forgive me. The words became Meg's mantra. Wiping the kitchen counter. Sorting laundry. While editing for the journal that offered her a part-time freelance job. A refrain, over and over, but interspersed with another lyric. Why not Joe?

Because she had a good life, that's why. A companionable marriage, the prospect of a comfortable old age, and kids, goddammit! To be with Joe would disrupt all of that. But did it have to? Couldn't she have it all? She'd never been audacious. What she was thinking wasn't impossible, though. Joe lived nearby. There was a pattern of visiting. It could be a secret. She remembered her grandmother telling her that every woman needed to have one enormous secret. "It's what gives a woman her sense of mystery, Megan. It's what allows her to look in the mirror, or in the faces of others, and say to herself, 'No one knows the real me, not really.'"

Meg looked in the mirror, pushed up her sagging cheeks. What was she thinking? She let her cheeks go, now faintly pink. She was thinking it might be good for her and Joe. And maybe for her and David, too.

"If there was a Make-A-Wish organization for dying adults," Rachel had piped up one day from a cloud of painkillers, "I'd have wished for a session with a really skilled lover. Someone young enough to go on forever, make me come at least four times."

Meg had choked back surprise but tried to be game since this is what Rachel seemed fixated on. "I've never heard you complain about Joe, Rach."

Her friend had plucked at the sheet. "No, he always had pretty good staying power. Maybe right now I'm just craving a great sword up the middle. Twenty-year-old sex to split me in two." She'd stopped talking then, perhaps realizing she'd crossed a line. Or had become exhausted by the process of staying alive. Meg was left with the images. She crossed and uncrossed her legs, then rose from the chair where she'd been holding vigil. "Can I get you some crushed ice?" she'd asked her friend.

What did staying power mean in Rachel and Joe's world, she wondered, and what words would she use to describe David if she were in Rachel's place? Generous? Loyal? But uninventive, too. No, this thing with Joe wasn't about better or different sex. This wasn't about sentimentalizing her youth or banishing boredom or mid-life discontent. It was about the years from fifty to eighty stretching out before her. About this being *her* time. Her "other side of menopause," as Rachel had put it. She didn't want to rely on Kyle and Carly to deliver the significant milestones anymore. Their marriages. Grandkids. This was the time for Meg—the Meg with life experience—to be someone other than wife, mother, caregiver, employee. She needed something—an enormous secret—to give her life some mystery.

DAVID KISSED HER CHEEK, pulling the blankets back over her as he rolled away. She wished him good morning. "Let's take Carly out for breakfast," she said, then regretted it. It was a suggestion based on mother-guilt when really, Carly was no fun to be with these days. Once Rachel had mumbled in a morphine haze, "Carly will always be your unknowable child, you know. You can ask her a million questions but will never know what's going on with her. She's one cool kid." Meg now understood what she'd meant. Carly hadn't fought for Meg's attention in the last two years. It gave her a small jolt. How had Rachel known Carly's temperament better than she had?

Later, watching Carly mop up egg yolk with toast, Meg asked her, "Are you sure Uncle Joe wants to play tennis this weekend?" It was her daughter's third egg. Her third piece of toast. And yet she was so slim and smooth-skinned. Her hair glowed with good health. Meg must have looked like that once, thirty years ago. All young people did. She'd been as confident of her attractiveness then as Carly seemed today. She'd missed the moment when her daughter had lost her adolescent uncertainty, her body and its gifts revealed to her. Maybe to others, too.

Carly dragged a serviette over her lips, then dabbed more delicately. "Why? What's the matter with getting back to tennis? And why are we still calling him Uncle Joe?" There was that edge to her voice again. Defensive. Combative.

"Nothing's the matter, sweetheart. I'm just surprised that Joe's feeling up to it."

"Why shouldn't he? He had lots of time to prepare for Rachel's death. It's not as if he hasn't been grieving for a while, Mom. I loved Rach, too, but we all knew what was coming."

"Carly." David laid a hand on his daughter's forearm.

"Okay," she said. "I should go. I have a paper to write. Thanks for breakfast, Dad. Mom, text me if you want me to drop off dinner at Joe's. Although you should stop doing that soon. It's kind of pathetic." She was gone in a second, leaving dust motes to twirl in the sun.

Meg straightened in her chair. "What did I say to set that off?"

David just shook his head. "When you're twenty-two, everything sounds like judgement. The instinct is to fight back."

"Were we like that, when we were her age?"

"Who knows. I think she's got a boyfriend, by the way."

Meg leaned sideways, forehead on palm. There'd been a time when that news would have made her happy, a time when she'd hoped to hear it from Carly herself over a pedicure. But now the sense of having failed her daughter just added to the impediments to moving on. Why was personal happiness so fleeting, so hard to grasp? What, dammit, was going to get her through if there was no real joy in her life? It seemed as though she was standing in sand, feeling the surf pressing in and pulling back, the tug in both directions. She looked at David, who was folding the pages of the newspaper into a smaller parcel. "Hey, are we ready for what's coming? Life will be so much less"—she searched for the right word—"fraught when Carly moves out. I'm afraid there will be nothing to mark the days with both kids gone. They'll all seem so quiet, with nothing to distinguish them."

He didn't look up. "Personally, I'm counting on it, Meg. But you..." His eyes met hers briefly. "You might want to take up tennis."

Joe wasn't expecting her, but she knew he'd be home. "I've come to do Rach's papers," she said, holding up a tray of takeout coffee, chocolate croissants peeking out of paper sleeves. She'd had a copy of the Paris photo ready to give him but left it in the car at the last minute.

She'd dressed carefully. Nothing too overtly different. No mascara, no lip colour. But with close attention to her clothes, the fit of them.

"I appreciate this, Meg. I should have been able to do this myself. I know it's mostly just lists, notes for this and that. But..." He took the coffee tray from her, placed it on the hall table and pulled her into a hug.

"I understand," she said. They'd hugged often over the years but, for the first time, she felt self-conscious. He had to be thinking about her last visit, as she was. But what was he feeling? She had no idea. Joe stroked Meg's shoulder blades. She pulled away. "Where should I start, then?"

He led her to the spare room. "The boxes are all in here." He opened the door but waited. She hadn't been in the spare room since the night of Rachel's death. It looked different. The hospital bed was gone, all the paraphernalia of sickness gone. Joe had set several bankers' boxes on the desktop, drawn back the cream curtains, and opened the window a few inches to let in the spring air. Outside, the trees' branches were still leafless—reaching grey arms and fingers—but Meg caught the trill of a red-winged blackbird, and the lyrics of an old folk song popped into her head. The melody had buoyancy to it. That was good.

"She'd gone through most of them, I think. When I opened one of the boxes the other day, there was a letter addressed to you on top. I guess she knew this would happen."

Joe turned away and disappeared down the hall. He'd already faced the ghosts in this room, the etched memory of the two of them holding on to Rachel's blueing hands. As Rachel's last breath had grated and receded, Meg had squeezed Joe's fingers hard, making them both cry out. They'd caught each other's eyes and something had passed between them so intimate and complicated she had yet to define it. Because in that moment, she told herself, only death was real. She flapped open the first box. A brown craft envelope lay on top. "For Meg," it read. "Open after I'm gone."

Meg sat back in the desk chair with its straight back, its businesslike mien. The chair rolled, and she pulled it back to the desk, pushing away the boxes to make space for whatever she was about to read.

There was only one page, in Rachel's handwriting, and another envelope, letter-sized, glued closed, but unaddressed.

> My dear Meg,
>
> I know you have done so much for me, and so I hate to ask you to do one last thing. Please send this envelope to the address below. Mike is an old friend. No, to be honest, Mike was more than an old friend. I met him at the gym. This may seem sordid to you right now. I'm sorry I could never explain. Please don't judge me. I never loved Joe any less because of it.
>
> You were <u>the</u> friend among friends. I hold you in my heart,
>
> R

Meg read and reread the note. It was as if she'd been hit by shock waves from a detonation. And from this destruction rose emotions that were easy to name. Surprise. Anger. At the end, at the very end, Rachel's thoughts had been on someone outside their triangle of grasping hands. On Mike, a perfect stranger to Meg, from the gym Rachel had attended for decades. Who was this person whose name had never passed Rachel's lips, even in innocent storytelling? When had he insinuated himself into her friend's life? And how could she have kept this secret from Meg? Fuck, Rachel, how could you?

But quick as the dust rose, it began to settle. She didn't need to question Rachel, because she knew the answer. Suddenly it was clear why Rachel's life had glittered in a way that Meg envied. But what she really wanted to know was how Rachel had managed this secret. How could she have maintained a happy married life and still managed it? Rachel, you could have told me, shown me how, her inner voice railed. But she had told Meg in the end, hadn't she? Told her, asked not to be judged and, in asking, implied no judgement in return.

The chair was suddenly too confining. Meg rose and, as she shoved Rachel's note and the white envelope into her purse, knocked one of the boxes off the desk, spilling its contents. Immediately, Joe was there, hand on the door frame. "Are you all right?" he asked.

She couldn't answer. As the last of the papers settled into stillness, Joe stepped forward. "I'm sorry, Meg, I shouldn't have asked you to do this." He moved closer, his lips—full and dry—too close.

She pulled her gaze away to break the connection. "No, it was my fault, I'm sorry. I was clumsy. Let me tidy up." She grabbed the box, bent down, and restacked the papers neatly inside.

Joe, perhaps sensing her need to hide her face, stayed still, his socked feet just within her peripheral vision.

Still on her haunches, a sheaf of papers in her hands, she reached over and wrapped an arm around his legs, pressed her forehead into his groin. Like a beggar, she thought, asking without asking. What kind of unformed person was she? He placed a hand on her head, making her humiliation complete. "Oh, Meg, you know we'd always regret it," he said. "This just comes from being sad." He stroked her hair. She felt like a child and it made her cringe. "It's time to move on," he added. "It's time we both moved on."

MEG VOWED TO STAY SOBER. "Are you okay?" David asked on her return. She answered yes, even though she felt like she was looking through a broken windshield, the safety glass smashed into a mosaic.

"Could you and Carly please fend for yourselves tonight?" she asked, and David nodded, saying, "Carly's not here."

"I need some time alone. I'll be in Kyle's room."

She slept and when she woke, she sat on the side of Kyle's bed. It was dark outside, late. The house was quiet. She felt safe on the twin bed but lonely, all the people she might have turned to wrapped up in her confusion. She rubbed her hands up and down her arms. How many times had she asked Rachel if she were cold, noticing the gooseflesh on her friend's thin skin?

"No, hon," Rachel had answered every time. "This robe is as warm as toast. Everyone should have a fur-lined brocade robe. It should be government issue, included as part of palliative care." Meg had often wondered where the robe came from. It had arrived in the mail, she remembered. She'd meant to ask Rachel or Joe but never did.

She smoothed the wrinkles in her clothes. She wanted that robe. She'd told Joe that she didn't want any of Rachel's clothes, but now she wanted that boudoir-inspired robe.

It was late, but not so late that she couldn't be forgiven for knocking on Joe's door and asking for it. He was a light sleeper, she knew, might even be awake. Carly's bedroom door was closed. She was either asleep or out. It didn't matter. Carly was an adult now.

The drive wouldn't take long, but her thoughts collided. She decided it might be better to walk. Fantasy? Foolishness? Every woman should have a secret, Grams had said. And Rachel's message had been clear: Joe should find someone right away. I am moving on, Joe, Meg argued with him now in her head. This is about moving on.

The house was lit. Turn back? No, the lights were a good omen. She kept walking. Front walk, front steps. The robe would feel warm, like skin against skin, so warm. Should she knock or ring? There were loud voices and music coming from inside. Joe? No, too noisy for just Joe. Were the boys home again?

She peeked through the sidelights by the front door. There he was. With someone else. Someone dancing in Rachel's robe. Someone young. So young it might have been Carly. But this person was laughing, spinning, bare-legged. Not grieving for Rachel, so it couldn't be Carly. Could it? Through ruched lace curtains, it was hard to tell.

She pulled back, spine straight, scalp tingling. What had made her think immediately that Joe was fucking her daughter? It had to be someone else. But where would Joe have met someone that young, and when could it have started? Her stomach heaved, made her fold in two at the waist. She was leaping to conclusions. Imagining that inside was someone young like Carly when all she'd seen was robe and legs and hair. Presuming more was going on than just a dance, two people having fun. What was abhorrent was the notion that Joe might have chosen someone younger over her. She'd never forgive him, if it were true.

She couldn't bring herself to look in those sidelights again. She was jealous: of Rachel and her well-kept secret, of Joe for laughing again already, and of whoever was inside—interfering with Meg's inept pursuit of her might-have-been.

The night was more humid than she'd expected, the kind of night that would green up the lawn overnight. Go home, Meg, she said to herself, turning away from the door, the light and liveliness pouring through the narrow windows. Go home to David. Stop peeking through Rachel's damn sidelights and go home.

# An Imitation of Grace

If she could crawl out of the bed without waking Ollie; if she could tug the mosquito net back into place without letting in an opportunistic bug; if she could step into the garden and let the rural silence wrap her like a sarong; if a tray waited on the porch table with thick, milky coffee in a thermos and sweet purple rice in a covered bowl—if all that happened, then maybe she could live through another day as a widow and not break down.

But if she jostled Ollie by mistake, or the mosquito net caught his foot so that he reached out and clung to her with his brown eyes open—Rupert's eyes in a child's face—then she would not be able to hold back. She would have to turn away and cry.

But she did make it, out of the bed and down the stairs and to the porch without waking her son. Putu was coming up the path, a tray held on her head with one hand and a plastic bag in the other. The girl's hips swayed gently beneath the loose cotton draped from her waist. Her posture was perfect. At fifteen, she had already mastered Balinese grace.

"*Selamat pagi,* Miss Wen," Putu said, lowering the tray.

"*Selamat pagi*, Putu." There was no point correcting the girl. Wen. Gwen. It was close enough.

"Look after Ollie-baby today, Miss Wen?"

"Yes, please, Putu." For a few extra rupiah on top of the rent her family collected, the girl played with Ollie every morning while Gwen went off by herself, sometimes to shop in the market, sometimes to sit in a temple, but usually just to walk between the rice paddies. She paid for this personal space to insulate her pain from erosion, from being pushed aside by others' needs—especially those of her toddler.

The coffee was more bitter than usual. She could hear Ollie and Putu in the upstairs room, Ollie asking, "Where's Mommy?" and Putu answering, "Soon, soon." The house was a simple cement structure with a dried grass roof—just a single bedroom above and a sitting area, porch, and bathroom below—but the garden had sold it. The morning after she and Ollie had settled in, she'd wandered the grounds and counted over a hundred distinct plants. She'd expected their mixed scents—frangipani and jasmine—to be calming.

In a few minutes, Putu and Ollie would come downstairs for breakfast. She knew what would happen next if she stayed on the porch. Ollie would leap onto her lap. At three, he was all sunshine once he was awake. He'd hug her with his chubby arms, snuggle his silky head under her chin. She'd be forced to smile or kiss him before she could place him firmly on the cushion next to her in order to escape.

His hugs and kisses—so wet and innocent—made her throat tense with resistance. She knew that the loss of Rupert should have made her cling to their child, knew that Ollie needed her time and attention and that Ollie's needs should trump her own. But guilt wasn't enough to make her want to be his mother. Her baby held no charm. It frightened her a bit.

She grabbed her bag and slipped to the side of the house, waiting there until Putu and Ollie descended and he was seated in a chair that faced away from the window.

"Po-widge?" he asked, already leaning toward the bowl Putu placed before him. The purple rice had not yet lost its novelty.

"Yes, and papaya fruit." Above his head, Putu caught Gwen's eye and Gwen waved her hands palm down in what she hoped was a universal sign not to reveal her presence.

"Papa-ya," Ollie said, testing the new vocabulary and causing the pit of Gwen's stomach to roil. Ollie had called Rupert Daddy, not Papa, but the word had clearly reminded him that his father was missing. His voice quavered.

Putu was unreadable. "Look, Ollie," she said, pulling a toy from the plastic bag she'd brought with her. Shaped like a ski hill, it came with a handful of plastic penguins that slid down the front and marched up the back on a battery-operated conveyer. Oblivious to the incongruity of this toy in a place where there was no snow or ice, no winter season at all, Ollie was momentarily distracted. As Gwen mouthed "thank you" to Putu, she wondered why the black and white toy had attracted the girl's attention in the first place. It reminded her that it would start to snow at home soon and that Christmas would follow. She stepped away from the window and called out, "I think I'll go to the Wi-Fi cafe for a while."

"No worries, Miss Wen."

"Mommy?" It was impossible to mistake Ollie's rising distress.

"Be good, Ollie," she called back, as the toy's motor kept running, moving the penguins up and down the plastic mountain.

SHE TUCKED HER SARONG around her knees and flipped open her laptop with reluctance. Today, like every day she'd checked her messages, there would be a backlog of condolences and queries from friends. And from her family, more questions. Where was she staying exactly? How was she? Didn't she realize that escaping to Indonesia with a toddler just after the funeral was considered an odd and irresponsible, if not downright crazy, thing to do?

Her sister Allison was the only one who understood. *I get it, Gwen. I get why you had to leave right away. Stay as long as you need to. It's damp and grey here anyway. I'm looking after the paperwork. Do you need more money?*

She was thankful for Allison, the only one of her family who wasn't asking her to explain. Truthfully, she had no good reason for what she'd done. Rupert's death had been so sudden, so senseless. Biking to work on a wet October day when a car had skidded and hit him, he'd been dead before Gwen had risen from their bed and showered. She'd gone through the next week in a trance, following the instructions of her mother, her brother, the businesslike benefits administrators she'd been referred to by her employer and Rupert's. Ollie had spent that whole week sitting next to her, stunned into quiet by the change in routine, by the constant presence of his mother, by her aloofness. Despite how detached she'd felt, there'd been no question of leaving him with his aunt or his grandmother. That conversation would have required too much effort. She'd packed a small bag for the two of them, transferred cash to her credit card, and left.

This morning, a message from Gwen's mother headed the list. *My dear Gwen, there is a process to grieving that you can't escape. It's been six weeks now. It's time to come home, for Oliver's sake.*

"Cremation today?" A man held out a ticket. Gwen shook her head. She'd already financed one this month, thanks, paid for by American Express just like any other transaction. She knew that in Bali the ritual cremations prized by the locals were expensive. It wasn't surprising that tourists were enlisted as donor-spectators. She'd encountered several processions in the past six weeks, caught between the mobile gamelan players and the tiered *wadah* tower used to transport the coffin to the cremation pyre. Each time, she'd run for the nearest store, hidden among the artwork and jewellery the Balinese were famous for, and bought small hand-carved frogs and geckos painted in primary colours while she waited for the procession to pass. Had she really been here six weeks already? She'd hardly noticed the passing of the days. Time for her was measured only in the blooming and fading of the flowers in her garden, the height of the rice stalks in the paddy beyond. What did it matter whether Ollie was here or home right now? Back home, they would have to eat off the dishes that Rupert had used, sleep in sheets he had slept in. Ollie would hardly notice these details, but she would. She needed this distance, this buffer from the truth. Ollie could wait until she was ready to go back. His surroundings didn't matter. He wouldn't remember any of this later.

She placed her fingers on the keyboard to prepare a response for her mother. Next to her, a woman leaned in toward her own laptop and yelled, "Fuck, Dave, are you telling me you're not coming at all?" The man framed in the screen turned his head so that he wasn't looking in the camera. "It's work, babe. I don't have any control over work," he said. "But you two stay and enjoy. It's all paid up."

"Like hell you don't have any control over work. You own the damn company! And you promised Luke and me we'd have a holiday together. You promised, Dave."

"Hey, some of us are trying to work here," said a guy sitting at the counter. Other cafe patrons looked with hostility at the woman. "Like I give a shit," she said to no one in particular and turned back to her laptop. Behind the counter, the owner of the cafe stopped wiping glasses, trying to gauge where the small crowd's anger might lead.

The woman hissed, "Who is she this time, Dave? Who is she? Never mind, I don't care. But you explain it to your son. You explain to Luke that some other woman is more important to you than two weeks with your own kid." She turned her head in Gwen's direction and yelled. "Luke, where are you? Come talk to your father." To Gwen she said, "Stay single. That's my advice. Lukey, get over here!"

Gwen hadn't noticed the boy. Maybe six, he was playing with a couple of toy cars near the cafe's back door. He looked up, not at his mother but directly at Gwen, with an expression so blank it took her breath away. How had a child already learned such control over his emotions? She wiggled her fingers goodbye at him, swept up her computer and was almost out the door when the boy said, "Hi, Daddy," sweetly, innocently, as if he'd been deaf to the commotion. Fooling no one.

"MONKEY FO-WEST!" Ollie demanded when Gwen returned to the porch. He never tired of the place.

"Okay, get in your stroller." It was a destination near enough to walk, but far enough to fill a good part of the day. Putu slipped away, plucking a fresh flower from the frangipani tree for her hair as she passed.

The bustle along Jalan Raya Ubud and Jalan Monkey Forest had already started—hundreds of motorcycles, cars, bikes, tourists, men with packages to deliver to open shops, women on their way to the temples with artfully complicated platters of rice and flower offerings on their heads. Gwen focused on the fronds of trees that leaned over the streets, the moss and other plants that filled every space not occupied by commerce. She wondered again whether the beauty of Bali could suck the hurt out of her—replace her shrivelled heart with something thrumming and alive.

Entering the forest was like entering a child's imagination. Maybe if she'd lived on the Pacific coast, with its old-growth rainforests, the place might have seemed less fantastical. But she was used to the orderly pines and maples in urban parks. Here, air roots hung from the high trees like walls. Statues surrounded her, so green with moss they seemed to sprout from the ground—demon-like, dog-like, winged and tailed.

"Well surprise, surprise. You have a kid, too." It was the woman from the Wi-Fi cafe, this time with a bored drawl rather than high-pitched accusations. "I thought you were one of the yoga junkies."

Gwen clicked open the safety belt that held Ollie in the stroller. "Go play, Ollie," she said, and when he seemed reluctant to move out of her orbit, added, "Look, there's another little boy here today. His name is Luke." She gestured at Luke, took in his stony face.

Ollie, caught between his desire to beeline for the nearest macaque and his interest in the older boy, hesitated before the monkeys finally won out. Gwen kept an eye on him; the adult macaques could be aggressive in their search for food—had stolen eyeglasses, hats, and necklaces from past visitors. Luke hung back, clutching his cars.

"I'm Andy," said his mother. "Andrea. I'm at the Viceroy. Where're you staying?"

The Viceroy was five-star: breathtaking and expensive. A place with private villas for honeymooners, like she and Rupert had been when they'd stayed there previously. "I'm renting a local place," said Gwen.

"You're not one of those women here to find yourself, are you? *Eat, Pray, Love* with a kid in tow?"

"No."

"Don't you wish we could lose the kids, just be single again for a while? Then this place would be amazing. The men are gorgeous. Hell, the women are gorgeous. I saw a bunch of them bathing in an irrigation ditch this morning, their sarongs all clingy, hiding nothing. Had to stop myself from jumping in with them and grabbing a boob."

Boob? What was the woman talking about now? It had all been noise after "lose the kids" and "be single." Gwen's inner voice had screamed, Yes! while also screaming, Get a grip. Of course not! She moved toward Ollie who was now surrounded by five or six sweet-faced young monkeys and several mothers, more feral-looking with their incongruous grey moustaches and droopy breasts. The gold-coloured primate eyes held human consideration but a hint of the demonic—mirrors to Gwen's own soul. Go ahead, take him, she silently challenged the closest mother macaque. Grab him and run! I'd never catch up.

As if reading her traitorous mind, Ollie slipped back to her, wrapped his arms around her thigh—afraid, in the way that all small children are intrinsically afraid, that she might disappear.

Andy trailed behind her. "Have you met that hottie, Wayan, at the Clear Cafe?"

Gwen shook her head. The woman obviously didn't know that something like one-third of the male servers at the Clear were named Wayan—that it roughly translated to first son. The locals played a game with it. "Ask for Wayan at the taxi stand," they'd advise unknowing tourists. She'd have liked to see Andrea fall for the trap. She'd already decided they could never be friends.

Undeterred by Gwen's silence, the woman spoke again. "I'm starved. Aren't you starved? Let's take the kids to get something to eat."

"I'm not really hungry."

"Come on. Food. Coffee. Liquor, if we can get it this early. Look, the boys have had enough. There's a decent place just outside the gates."

It was true that Luke had barely moved since they'd arrived. Ollie was watching the monkeys pester a pack of tourists who had come to the forest with bananas and coconuts. Maybe if she went with this annoying woman, she could make some excuse to slip away for a few minutes on her own. She could tell her she needed to buy tampons—something the woman couldn't refuse her.

"Look, it's my treat. If I'm going to be stuck here for two weeks by myself, I'd better meet some people other than restaurant employees. Come on, Ollie, we're going for fries. What's your name, anyway?" she asked Gwen as she turned toward the exit, confident they'd all follow. Ollie was already at her heels, fries being the magic word. If he started repeating it, as he often did, Gwen imagined she might pinch him. She could already feel the soft squish of his flesh.

"I'm Gwen," she said, reluctantly falling in behind.

They filed into the cafe closest to the Monkey Forest, the place where Gwen and Ollie usually had a late lunch after the midday crowds had moved on. The large family that owned the cafe always made them feel welcome. They seemed to understand Gwen's need for respite and often whisked Ollie away to their family compound in the back so she could drink her final coffee in peace. Today Gede smiled as they entered, but his face showed surprise when he realized she was with Andrea.

"Four Cokes," Andrea demanded before they'd even sat down. "And fries, lots of them." She patted her flat stomach. "Why bother looking good when husbands just cheat anyway?"

Gwen shook her head. "Ollie will have fruit juice," she said, and Gede nodded.

Ollie clambered up onto a chair. "And rambutans," the boy pronounced, enunciating carefully. Gede had introduced him to this new favourite fruit.

"Rambo-what?" Andrea asked, but no one bothered to answer. Luke stared out the window, occasionally glancing back at Gwen, but studiously avoiding his mother. His eyes, which angled down naturally at the outer edges, made him look like an unhappy clown. Gwen sensed that he was very sad, was holding in that sadness the same way she was holding in her own. At what age was true sadness possible? True understanding of loss, the finality of it? Ollie was too young, but Luke seemed to perceive that his family was broken, his father to remain distant, either physically or emotionally or both. Six was too young to know such mournfulness. The next time Luke glanced at her, Gwen tried to smile. The muscles were out of practice.

A crowd was gathering outside in the street. Gamelan music and gongs heralded yet another funeral procession. The metallic music was lovely when it accompanied a traditional dance or was played softly in the background at a restaurant. For the funeral, it seemed more discordant or was intentionally so. It triggered a recurring vision of Rupert's muscular body consumed by flames—a choice he'd written down but never communicated to her directly. She shivered.

"Someone walk on your grave?" Andrea asked.

"Why can't you just leave—" Gwen whispered. Any semblance of healing she'd experienced since arriving in Bali had completely disappeared. It felt as if air wasn't reaching her lungs, was stalled somewhere in her windpipe.

"What?" Andrea asked. "I couldn't hear you over that infernal noise."

Gede placed a plate of ripe rambutans in front of Ollie and disappeared with a nod. The fruits looked like small red hedgehogs. The boy began to rip away the spiky outer armour of the largest one.

"Is it possible to get some rum for this Coke?" Andrea called out to the now empty cafe before turning back to Gwen. "So, is there a husband or ex-husband or what?" she asked.

Heat washed over Gwen's body, the flush that preceded fainting. She concentrated on Ollie's progress. He'd exposed the rambutan's flesh, opaque and pearly white.

"Excuse me. I have to go to the bathroom. Gede?" she called. He reappeared with a quick, dismissive glance at Andrea. "Could you or your sister please mind Ollie for a minute?" She stayed nearby just long enough to watch the young man place four shot glasses of rum on the table and hold out a hand to her son, another to Luke.

The bathroom, like so many Balinese living spaces, was open to the air, made private by a wall of plants. Gwen kicked off her flip-flops and dug her toes into the smooth decorative pebbles that covered the floor, searching for one sharp edge that would cause a neutralizing pain, make her panic recede. She splashed cold water on her face, forcing herself to breathe as she looked in the mirror and practiced the answer that she would have to give over and over, for the rest of her life. "He died. He's dead."

"Where's Luke? Lukey?" Andrea's scream cut through the cafe and drew Gwen from the bathroom. She'd lost track of time—the

Coke and shot glasses were empty. Andrea stood alone, her trim body rigid but swaying, a hand out to steady herself. "Where did that man take Lukey?" she yelled across the room.

"It's okay. Gede probably took him to the kitchen. Stay here. I'll get him." Gwen was thankful for the excuse not to return to the table. She headed to the cafe's back door, which opened to the family compound. There, Ollie and Gede's sister sat cross-legged on one of the kitchen platforms, cooking chunks of meat on a brazier. Below the platform, Luke's cars lay abandoned.

Ollie looked over at her, his cheeks rounding then softening as he sensed no lasting attention from his mother. With a tremendous effort, Gwen touched his head, struggling to hide her inner turmoil, her inability to process the tragedy that had left her alone with this child. And now Luke was missing. At least this time, Ollie's innocence, his inculpability in the face of these events, did not repulse her. He was just a baby. Hers and Rupert's. She hefted his warm body from the platform, kissed both his eyes. "Honey, I have to look for Luke. You stay here with Ketut, okay? I'll be back to get you soon. I promise, I'll be back."

Ketut leapt to her feet, panicked to realize that the other boy had gone missing while in her care, but Gwen handed her Ollie, signalled for her to mind her cooking. "It's not your fault," she said. "Don't worry. I'll find him."

Neither Andrea nor Gede were in the cafe when she re-entered. Another sibling or cousin stood by the door, holding a tray of coffees destined for a new group by the window. He gestured, spoke quickly. Gede was already out looking, she gathered.

The funeral procession had passed. It would be headed toward the crossroads, where the men carrying the coffin in its fanciful tower would spin it around to prevent the spirit from finding its way home. It had a long way to go before reaching the cremation grounds—must be for someone of local importance to take this route. To Luke, it had probably looked like a parade, a place to hide and to be entertained at the same time.

The trailing end of the procession was not far off, and Gwen slowed to survey the crowd for Luke from a few metres behind. There was nothing formal about these Balinese ceremonies. Full of ritual, yes—flowers and incense and deeply held beliefs about the need to return the spirit to the elements—but without stiff reserve. The men and women in the procession chatted among themselves, called out to people ahead and behind. They were not dressed up. Gwen, in a long lacy blouse that fell below her hips, a cotton sarong and sash, and the plastic flip-flops that she'd bought in a street market, was dressed just like all the other women. The men wore collared shirts or black tees with their sarongs, some advertising local shops and websites, others faded to a slate grey. Only the gamelan players had some semblance of costume, their sarongs a matching plaid.

As the group pressed forward haphazardly, Gwen joined them and threaded her way closer to the men now straining beneath the *wadah*. They were boisterous and loud, swinging the tower from side to side, their role—to confuse the spirit—an occasion for good fun. The gathering after Rupert's funeral had been a mostly silent affair, crowded with friends, cousins, and aunts and uncles stunned by the need to come together again just four years after Gwen and Rupert's wedding in the same church. "Where's the body?" Rupert's aged grandmother had asked in the thin, high-pitched voice of the hearing impaired, and someone had answered equally loudly, "Rupert asked to be cremated." The old lady hadn't let it go. "But no one in our family has ever been cremated," she said.

Gwen was now among men and women with roughly torn white cotton strips around their foreheads or tied to their ponytails—perhaps the closer relatives. She hadn't seen these symbolic bands before, but the caste of the deceased and village traditions made each ceremony different. Not one in the group was crying or red-eyed. Not one clutched a tissue or draped a consoling arm around another. When an older woman caught Gwen's eye, they both nodded.

She spied Luke ahead of the tower, walking beneath the long white cloth that unfurled from its front, held up by those in the lead. She supposed it gave the child the illusion of cover, or perhaps he found it cooler in its shade. She held out a hand, called, "Luke! It's time to go." He ran to her and took her hand just as the leaders began to fan out on a rough field, a broken soccer net at one end. It was a detail that would have offended at home but was irrelevant here. She drew the boy off to the side where they stood and watched as women laid out platters of offerings on makeshift tables and men manoeuvred the coffin from the tower to a spot closer to the pyre. They stayed standing as the men removed the shrouded body from the coffin.

"We need to go back to the cafe. Your mom is worried about you," Gwen said.

Luke ignored her. "Is that a dead person?" he asked.

"Yes." There was no point lying.

"Are they going to burn it?"

"Yes."

"I wish my mom and dad were dead."

She looked down at him. He was angry and hurt, but perhaps she'd been wrong to presume he understood loss and its finality. When he looked up at her, she said nothing; it wasn't her place to be shocked or to cajole him with platitudes about love.

A man stepped forward to perform another complicated ritual of prayer while using a flower to dash water on the corpse. Gwen thought she could smell jasmine but knew she was too far away. It was as if the scent suddenly rose from her skin.

"They're going to light the fire soon, Luke." Several men lay metal pipes from the pyre to gas canisters that were set at a distance.

"I know. I want to see." For the first time, his voice was animated.

"Okay." She dropped his small hand and crouched to put an arm around his shoulders. In the milling crowd, a young woman held up a photo in a frame but Gwen couldn't tell if the picture was of a man or a woman. She imagined it was a man. But when tears pricked her eyes, she imagined it was a flower, a huge lotus in a tight ball that would open, petal by petal, in response to the sun's heat. As the fire began to build, the gas fuelling it made a rushing sound. The air around the pyre blurred and, again, Gwen thought she would faint.

Luke suddenly curled into her. His shoulders shook, but when he pulled away to speak, his eyes were dry. "We should go find Ollie," he said. "He'll want his mommy."

She nodded and rose from her crouch to look one last time at the hundreds of people milling in front of her. Beyond the soccer field, rice paddies rose in layers that cut into the rolling hills, sparkling blue pools next to swaths of emerald green. The local people had lived with their lush surroundings so long that she wondered if they saw this landscape the way she did, or just accepted its beauty, as they apparently accepted death.

From across the field, she saw Gede wave, saw Andrea's shoulders sag in relief. The plaintive scent of jasmine still wafted around her as she led Luke toward them, away from the heat of the fire. The soft cotton of her sarong swung loosely from her hips. Tentatively, consciously, she let all her joints loosen—swayed her hips just a little from side to side—in what she hoped was a good imitation of Balinese grace.

# Lost Language

The corner where she'd been told to wait smelled like car exhaust, urine, and stale French fries. The cement wall next to the subway exit had a cold grip on Ali's spine. She triple-checked Jake's instructions on her phone, then zipped it back into the top compartment of the backpack she'd rested by her feet. Her hiking boots still looked new, even though she'd had them for three years. She wriggled her toes and wished she'd brought lighter shoes for the drive. Damp, sweaty socks would be uncomfortable when they left the park gate for the backcountry.

The car that pulled up at seven thirty was exactly what she'd been told to look for: an old, navy Subaru Forester scratched along the length of the passenger's side. There were three people inside but only Jake, the trip leader and driver, got out to meet her. He popped the hatch so she could stuff in her pack, and she was relieved that hers was no bigger or smaller than the others and had about the same wear and tear. It took a few minutes to put her snowshoes and poles in the car's rooftop cargo box, she and Jake both jostling to be helpful and only getting in the way of each other.

Once they were both in the car, Jake made perfunctory introductions. Pete in the front passenger seat and Tara in the back looked up from their phones, nodded, said hi, then withdrew their attention again. Ali didn't miss the grey-blue glow of her screen, but she wished she had something to fiddle with instead. A pen and notebook, maybe. Or a book, if it had the right title.

The car rattled and vibrated as if it hadn't warmed up yet. Jake placed his hands on the wheel at precisely ten and two. He checked his mirrors and glanced around to make sure that all three of his passengers were wearing their seatbelts. "All set, then?" he asked, and without waiting for an answer added, "We should be there in about four hours. It takes forever just to get past the suburbs."

ALI HAD FORGOTTEN what it felt like to sit in a backseat for so long. Three hours in, she sipped the cooling coffee in her Thermos and nibbled on the sandwich she'd brought along for the ride. Jake had warned that he'd make only one coffee and bathroom stop on the way up, and she didn't want to have to ask for a second. Conversation among the group—brief, staccato outbursts at best—had waned after the first half-hour. Both Pete and Tara were now tipped sideways against the windows with their eyes closed, asleep or pretending to be.

Despite the disinterest in talking, it was clear that the other three knew each other. When asked, Ali confirmed this trip was her first with the Singles Outdoor Club but that she'd done a lot of winter camping with her dad and canoe-tripping camps in the summers growing up. She made a point of mentioning that her father had been a backcountry guide and had taught her how to take care of herself in the outdoors. If the others had any concerns she'd slow them down or be improperly equipped, she thought she'd addressed them.

What they hadn't asked—and Ali was grateful—was: Why this trip and with this club instead of friends? She wondered if there was some etiquette that discouraged too much prying when someone new joined, or maybe the others just assumed she was there for the same reasons they were. Even though times had changed, and people overshared all the time, Ali didn't think she was ready to explain the catastrophic thinking that had plagued her since she'd moved to the city to be an editor. In her one-room apartment, she couldn't remember the musky scent of wet fields and imagined them paved over, all the forests near her home cut to beard stubble. When she reported to her therapist that the language of natural things was disappearing from her lexicon, he suggested she make a weekend visit to a park. She'd agreed but turned down his offer to book a follow-up appointment. He hadn't taken her seriously when she told him that, in a moment of pure panic, she'd had to look up the spelling of sky, certain it contained a silent fourth letter.

Jake's car juddered on a rumble strip, and Ali caught him checking her out in the rearview mirror. She still hadn't got a good look at anyone else in the car. She turned to stare out the window, twisting her neck to try to catch the name on a sign announcing a First Nation. The only one she remembered was the Wahta Mohawks, once known for growing cranberries. Each time her family had passed the sign advertising their fruit store,

Ali's mom had suggested stopping to buy fresh berries, but her dad never took the turnoff, eager to carry on driving north. Now the business was closed. Instead, there were new shops along the highway selling smokes, bait, gas, and doughnuts. Ali tasted the names of these communities on her tongue—Magnetawan, Shawanaga, and Dokis—wondering how much the Indigenous names had been changed to fit the English syllabics.

"Did you say something?" Jake broke the silence, speaking to her in a low voice so as not to disturb the others.

"No, sorry," she said, touching the tips of her fingers to her lips as if to remind herself to be wary. She must have been whispering aloud. She wondered if it had become a habit, another consequence of living and working alone. She wondered if she should get a cat to make her muttering acceptable, although evidence suggested a houseplant might be better. She'd read somewhere that plants responded well to human conversation.

It was after eleven when Pete and Tara began to rouse and stretch. Jake pulled into the park's unloading zone and began delegating tasks before he'd even switched off the ignition. Ali hoped he wasn't going to behave like a Boy Scout troop leader the entire weekend. That the others didn't bristle at the orders seemed a good sign. Jake had been driving for a long time. He was probably just eager to enjoy the outdoors—what they'd all come for.

Tara and Jake strode off to the gatehouse to get permits, leaving Ali and Pete to unload. Ali got her first good look at Pete's face as the two of them wrestled the packs from the back of the car and unloaded the snowshoes. His eyes were different colours—one blue, one hazel, hard to decide which to look at—and there was a raised scar down the right side of his face. Ali thought he and Tara might be related. They both had full bottom lips and long, narrow faces. After another covert look at Pete's profile, she decided probably not. It was just their expressions that gave the impression of similarity: rigid cheeks and tense foreheads. They looked worried, but then she probably did too.

The scar made her curious—who wouldn't be curious?—but these days it was easy to offend, and there were risks to asking questions. Safer to stay silent and focus on the tasks at hand. Although silence had a downside too. All the scary shit that filled the vacuum.

Pete pulled a small tube from the pocket of his jacket and began to rub sunscreen on his face. SPF 60, she noticed, pretty strong for March. He offered Ali the tube. She shook her head.

"Did you bring a tent?" he asked, and she shook her head again. "No, I have a bivy sack."

"Do you want to leave it behind? I have a double. Tara will be sharing with Jake."

"Oh. Are they together?"

Pete shrugged. "Up to you. Doesn't mean anything. Just a way to reduce weight."

She considered the bivy, cramped and awkward when it came to dressing and undressing. She started to open her pack to remove its stuff sack and the groundcover that went with it. "You sure?" she asked.

He nodded, not looking at her, and opened his hands wide, palms raised, in a gesture she didn't understand.

THEY WERE ON their way, Jake leading, the rest of them a short distance behind like a clutch of ducklings. Ali was more adept and balanced on her snowshoes than she expected, the weight of her pack stabilizing her on the short downhill that took the group to the first lake. Jake stopped at the shoreline and waited for the others to catch up.

"Ice is thick, twenty-five centimetres at least. Just in case, Pete and I have ropes. Any questions?"

They all stood silent until Jake headed off. For a long time, there was just the sound of four pairs of shoes squelching across the ice, the squeak and caw of poles planted in and then pulled from the thin coating of snow. Ali concentrated hard, but there was nothing else to hear, no bird sounds, no bark crackling in the trees, not even the distant purr of an airplane, although she could see fresh contrails overhead. She begged for some message of welcome from the land, but all she heard was air across her eardrums.

They walked down the centre of the crescent-shaped lake, headed for a summer canoe portage that would take them to a more distant lake, where they would camp. Thirty minutes in, Tara stopped and pointed at fresh tracks ahead.

"Fox," Jake said, though Ali thought the prints looked bigger than that.

The presence of wildlife didn't seem to excite the others in any way. They'd perked up a little since they'd set out, but no one effused over the landscape or the weather or how lucky they were that they had all 645 square kilometres of park to themselves, according to the gate attendant. This information had been passed along by Jake as if it held the same significance as where to park the car or who would be responsible for their garbage. Being new, Ali had volunteered to take the yellow plastic bag. But she couldn't bring herself to be the one to start a conversation, even though the surroundings called out to be admired—the sky a clear, vibrant blue, the cedars that rimmed the lake popping olive green against the smoky haze of the birches. After she'd taken in her surroundings, she gazed down, trying to describe in her mind the texture of the snow that coated the ice. She thought if she could come up with the perfect description, she might try it out on the others. But too many possibilities seemed trite: slushy, crinkly, rippled, like a quilt, like a cloud. She gave up, leaning over to scoop a handful of the crystals into her mouth, liking the crunch, the metallic taste of it against her tongue.

When she and her dad had gone winter camping, he'd always given Ali the job of collecting snow and boiling it to make hot drinks—hot chocolate, or Irish coffee when she'd got a little older. He'd pull out a small silver hip flask, untwist the cap and, with a wink, tip a generous ounce into each of their cups. The tales he'd tell over the campfire of past mishaps were always laced with disparaging humour and lessons he'd wanted her to learn: don't pitch a tent downwind of a sparking fire; always, always carry matches and a knife; and don't rely on anyone else to read a map. He was a different person on those trips, garrulous and funny and confident in his skills, not the man who grunted hello to her friends as he flopped on the couch and turned on the TV. And she was different, too, opening up with him about her dreams of a writing job as the two of them used shallow creeks to race twigs dipped in pine sap.

She'd loved family camping trips and missed with a hollow wordlessness her dad's eagerness to teach her about the outdoors. He'd died in such a stupid way, hitting his head on a low-hanging branch as he'd turned to watch her mother manoeuvre her kayak through some white water. Ali hadn't been on that trip, and now her mom wouldn't talk about it, only saying she was done with all that.

When Ali eventually looked up, the group had spread out in front of her, their shoes leaving trails behind them of vaguely ovoid impressions, grey on grey, in a fan-like array. She knew nothing about these people, despite the hours they'd now spent together, not even how they were shaped under their layers of fleece and Gore-Tex. Tara had said so little that if Ali were asked to identify her voice tomorrow, she couldn't be sure she would recognize it. She'd presumed a singles outdoor club was a way for shut-in city dwellers to strike up new relationships when really it was turning out to be a bunch of introverts searching for something they didn't—or couldn't—talk about. Like her, the others were of the generation brought up to believe there were places where the grass was greener but whose reality made them increasingly uncertain of getting there. Ali had talked in circles about it with her therapist, knowing that her greatest fear was all too easy to put into words—that *there* might cease to exist in her lifetime.

She stopped walking and pushed against her diaphragm with flat palms to force a sense of calm. She'd made it this far, hadn't she? They all had—to this wide open space. But ahead of her, the others were strewn across the ice, silent, great distances apart.

THEY WENDED THEIR WAY through trees, sidestepping up a high hill. On the steep downside, the snow had softened in the weak afternoon sun. Every three or four steps, their snowshoes would punch through the surface, slowing them down, and both Ali and Tara got caught in tree wells, leaving them up to their thighs in snow. They had a hard time pulling up and out of these holes. They crawled on hands and knees like turtles under their awkward packs, hauling themselves upright using tree trunks. Ali was tired when they finally arrived at the campsite Jake had picked, a small island with a view of the park's famous white quartzite cliffs.

Beneath a stand of trees near the island's centre, some windswept ground covered in dry pine needles made a good place to pitch their tents. Jake sent Tara and Ali to collect firewood and water from a running stream while he and Pete began to prep the evening meal.

In closer quarters, the smell of sweat and damp wool wafted from their clothes. Ali took off her gloves to slap her hands together to warm them, and the scent of pine pitch rose from her fingers. They still weren't talking, but at least they were working together, had common goals.

After dinner, the group dispersed—to unpack, to brush teeth, to find a place to pee. Ali almost bumped into Pete, who was leaning against a tree trunk looking at the waning light of sunset.

"Are you okay?" she asked, and he nodded.

"Really, this shouldn't be so hard, should it?" he said.

"Winter camping?"

He looked at her in the dimness. "I don't want to have to herd my happiness into a corner to catch it. Do you know what I mean?"

She wasn't a hugger. She wasn't good at finding the right thing to say. She said, "Why don't we make a campfire?"

IT TOOK ALL FOUR OF THEM to get a flame to catch, each trying a bit of paper, a clump of fire starter, dry cedar. Tara began to worry aloud that they wouldn't have enough lighter fluid until both Ali and Pete drew matches from their pockets.

Darkness settled around them as they perched on fallen logs. Ali inhaled deeply, the resinous aroma of the burning pine somehow opening her up so that when she inhaled again she felt closer to the others, even though no new confidences had been exchanged. They were all in dark outerwear and only their faces were distinct in the firelight, floating like so many Cheshire cats without the grins. When the wind gusted, Ali felt the need to turn and look behind. There were spirits out there peering from the forest, she was sure. Ancients, seeing what she could not.

"It smells so good." Tara's voice broke the silence; all eyes spun toward her.

Ali hesitated, then plunged. "What is it about that primitive scent of a smoking fire that's so comforting?" Her agreement seemed to open a floodgate of observations from the others.

"Did you see that flock of geese fly overhead when we first hit George Lake?"

"Those tracks by the creek... I think they were beaver. Did

you notice where they dragged their tails?"

"No matter how often I come here, I'm still wowed by the quartzite cliffs. They almost make me want to be a climber."

The comments went on, neutral, then positive. Their sentences lengthened and organized. Ali shifted to warm one shoulder, then the other, turning to face each speaker. In their centre, the fire blazed, embers rising in spirals like miniature Tourbillion fireworks, writhing golden worms that beckoned and loosened their tongues. Like the embers, their enthusiasm exploded. They loved this park. This park was a jewel. Shouldn't they all return together in the summer, volunteer to do trail repair, check portages for deadfall, anything they could to preserve it for the future?

They agreed they should. The fire died down. They fumbled off to the two tents, Ali so tired she crawled into her sleeping bag almost fully dressed.

IN THE NIGHT, Pete shook Ali awake. "You're talking in your sleep."

"What?" She flailed, half awake, hitting him in the face by mistake, hoping the flesh under his scar wasn't still tender. "Sorry. I'm so sorry."

"You keep muttering. Place names from along the highway."

She had a fleeting memory of a dream. The Magnetawan. The Temagami. Other rivers she'd canoed as a teen with names that had once slid off her tongue.

"I'll roll over."

"It's okay. Listen a minute," he said.

The sounds were close, long drawn-out notes followed by

a few yips and then a response in a lower tone. “Oh.” Ali sighed her delight.

“Those tracks on the ice were from wolves.”

“Yeah, I knew what they were. There must be two packs. They’re talking, sharing stories.”

Pete lay back down beside her. Ali was warm now from the combined heat of two bodies inside the tent. A few minutes later, she could tell from his deep, conscious breaths that Pete still hadn’t fallen back to sleep, but the silence between them didn’t feel awkward anymore. They were past first words.

She took off her glove and placed her hand on the ground beyond her sleeping pad. Against her bare fingers, she felt the ground buzz. Close by, the trees murmured. The wolves shared their wisdom, while watchers whispered on the air. It was all still here.

# Memento Mori

When Lea described what happened, she said the sound of the bird striking the window was like a sharp clap, and her body lifted off the couch in alarm. She didn't say the sound was like gunshot because she'd never heard real gunshot and couldn't be sure how it sounded. She tried to be honest, even though the difference between what was remembered and actual experience was sometimes elusive. By then, she'd concluded she should cling to honesty, especially with herself.

And because she was trying to be honest, she also explained why she'd been lying on the sofa when the bird struck the glass. She'd just returned from the hospital, where she'd expected to pick up her mother, who was ready for discharge after being cured of an infection. Instead, she'd found her mom curled into a tight comma, unable to speak or move her limbs. "Maybe she had a stroke," said the nurse. Despite Lea's plea that she page a doctor immediately, the nurse appeared in no hurry to make the call.

IT WASN'T THE FIRST BIRD to hit the window, which was high up in Lea's living room near the cathedral ceiling, too high to reach even by ladder. Lea wasn't sure how many other birds there had been. A lot. Every time she heard the telltale smack, she resolved to attach stickers shaped like owls or raptors to deter birds from flying into the glass. But then she forgot about the stickers until the next time she heard a collision.

She always dreaded stepping outside, knowing she would find the bird in the driveway, either dead already or worse—stunned, broken, and in the throes of death. She usually waited an hour, knowing that she didn't have it in her to put the creature out of its misery, hoping that an hour was enough time for the bird to either gather itself and fly away or expire. While she waited, she was imaginative enough to contemplate how someone with more compassion or fortitude might end the bird's life mercifully, but the thought of holding it under water in a bucket or braining it with a loose brick made bile rise in her throat. This was the reason she'd never owned a cat or dog. Inevitably, it would come to the point where the animal would have to be euthanized. Ending the life of a creature in pain was something responsible pet owners did.

AFTER LEA FOUND a more sympathetic nurse, she was able to get a doctor to perform an examination of her mother. He gently but firmly manipulated her body so that it uncurled and straightened out, then scratched the soles of her feet, raised her arms and let them fall back on the bed, and peered into her eyes with a penlight. He ordered a scan, checked his phone, and said he'd know more later. Although he never introduced himself, he twice asked Lea to confirm her relationship to the patient before inquiring whether Lea's mother had prepared any advanced directives or signed a DNR order. Lea said her mom had assigned her power of attorney for personal care, and the documents were safe at home in her office. She did not tell the doctor her mom's clear wish not to be a burden to Lea or that she didn't want to be institutionalized for her personal care or have any tube inserted down her throat to keep her alive. This was information Lea had filed away mentally, hoping she would never have to act on it. Instead, she told the doctor she would sit at the bedside until the test results were ready.

Throughout this interaction, Lea smoothed her mom's flyaway hair, trying to make her look well-groomed, as if her mother had plans for the day. The permed hair was dyed chestnut, and although her mother had dyed it for so many years Lea couldn't remember the real colour, she planned to cut off a curl using the pair of scissors on the bedside table as soon as the doctor was gone. She'd tuck the curl in her purse, in the spare envelope she always kept there.

Her mom's dark eyes stayed fixed on the ceiling, and Lea was tempted to poke her into showing some sign of life so that the doctor would stop speaking in grievous tones about the likelihood of extensive brain damage. This, he said, would make a full recovery improbable, even if her mother survived the next few days. When the nurse flicked the curtain closed around the bed as the two left, Lea winced at the rattle of the hangers on the metal rod. Her mom's face seemed so hairless and youthful compared to her own. She ran a finger along the cheekbones and murmured, "I'm so sorry, Mom. I know this is not what either of us wanted for you." The only thing she could think to do was swipe one of her own lipsticks across her mom's dry, parted lips. But the colour was wrong; mother and daughter did not share the same skin tone.

ALTHOUGH LEA WAITED more than an hour before going outside to check, the bird still wasn't dead. It lay on its back, its wings folded tight against its body, blinking eyes glistening like hematite. It was a large bird, a northern flicker, with black dots on sandy breast feathers, a smooth, grey nape, black bib, and bright orange underwings and tail feathers.

This was the closest Lea had ever been to a flicker, although she'd heard them often. They were a nuisance bird, wily and destructive, with a strong beak for pecking. She'd never appreciated that flickers also had such glorious decoration, some feathers so vibrantly pumpkin they seemed unnatural for a bird. It gave it nobility—a value she hadn't perceived in it before.

The creature shuddered as Lea leaned in, alive but clearly dying. Blood flowed in a thin line between the rough nubbins of cement where it lay. Lea wanted her feelings for the bird to be unambiguous. A flicker—probably this flicker—had been damaging her house's woodwork for some weeks, damage that would be costly to repair. It would be easy to be indignant. She wanted to feel as if this bird had got what it deserved. Instead, she couldn't take her eyes from its spotted breast and colourful plumage. Observed so closely she could see the pen-sketch precision of the vanes' alignment in each feather, its life seemed worthy of preserving.

THE RESULTS OF THE SCAN were relayed to Lea before she left the hospital. The stroke was massive, the brain damage considerable. There was no point attempting surgery. The window for such efforts had closed and the bleeding would continue. Lea sat with this news, wondering whether the nurse who'd been so slow to call for a doctor had made her decision knowingly. She was young, and eighty-five years might have seemed like a full life to her, the effort to extend it futile.

Sometime later, a different doctor stopped by on his rounds. "Go home," he said to Lea, his eyes on the chart he held in front of his body like armour. "Get some rest. There may be some difficult decisions to make in the days ahead."

SHE GATHERED SHEETS OF NEWSPAPER in which to wrap the bird and rubber gloves to cover her hands. Handsome as it was, the thought of touching a dead bird repelled her.

Her thigh muscles ached from squatting low to the ground, and her eyes had a dry, gritty feel as if she'd stopped blinking. Every now and then, there was a weak flutter of wings, which were now relaxed away from the bird's body, exposing more fully the brilliant orange.

"Don't die, don't die, don't die," Lea whispered, even as her fingers hovered over those striking feathers. She wanted one but without having to pluck it or cause the bird more pain. She wanted something she could remember it by after she'd placed its newsprint-wrapped body in the green bin with all the other debris destined to decompose. She knew that by the next day she would not be certain if the colour of its tail feathers was closer to that of an orange or a carrot. The memory of their magnificence would fade.

LEA'S FATHER WAS ALSO DEAD. He'd had an ischemic stroke the year before. In the days after it happened and before he died, Lea and her mother had filled the hours with a conversation that went back and forth between wild hope and resignation.

"The doctor says your dad can't swallow effectively. He can't eat."

"They can put a tube down his nose. His swallowing might come back."

"I'm not sure this is what your father would want."

"We should ask about the other tube, the one that's inserted surgically."

"They've already put in a catheter. He'd find that so undignified. He'd hate it, if he knew."

"It's temporary, Mom. Why aren't they getting him up out of bed? He should have physio for mobility. He doesn't even have any facial droop."

"The doctor mentioned 'comfort care.' I'm confused about how that's different from palliative care. He's had a good life, your dad."

"Mom, he's fighting to live, I know he is. He raised his eyebrows when I talked to him. He tried to lift the blanket when I said I wanted to take him outside in a wheelchair. We can't give up on him."

Lea had never had any doubt that her parents loved one another. When her mom looked off into the distance, she recognized a lifelong habit of gathering her thoughts before responding. Lea herself might never know the delicate conversations that took place between older people who'd lived together as long as her parents—how they discussed and prepared each other for their inevitable deaths. But she knew her parents shared a strong belief that they should not burden their child.

"Your father has always been a strong, proud man. He could put up with a lot, but not with relying on anyone to feed him or clean his privates. It's not something either of us would like. So if it came down to that, I'd want you to let me go. So would he."

Lea's mother nodded with a sharp satisfaction as she swiped a cloth across the table between them with a hand that was lined but still firm. Lea looked at her mom—fully dressed, made up, and looking ten years younger than her age—and believed she would die as determinedly and with as little fuss as she'd lived.

She grabbed her mother's hand to stop her wiping. "I would clean your privates, Mom," she said.

LEA'S NEXT DOOR NEIGHBOUR stood at the end of her drive ready to haul in her garbage bin. "Everything all right?"

"I've failed at basic conservation measures."

The woman sauntered over to look down on Lea and the bird. "Oh, too bad. I was able to save a Steller's jay once."

Lea thought she caught an undertone of judgement. The newspaper she'd laid out to wrap the bird in seemed crass. She wished she'd chosen something different—colourful tissue or a sheet of gift wrap from the supply she kept in the basement. She crumpled the rubber gloves and stuffed them under her thigh.

The woman reached out to stroke the bird with an ease that made Lea flush. "I hope the poor thing didn't suffer."

THIS DOCTOR WAS THE FOURTH Lea had met at the hospital. "Did you and your mother discuss what she wanted before this event? Did she have any advanced directives?" he asked.

Lea knew her duties and responsibilities: to comply with her mother's expressed wishes if it was reasonable to do so, to guard her mother's best interests, and to act honestly and in good faith. The first lie felt like a rip through her chest. "No," she said. "Mom wasn't clear on a situation like this."

"Well, we can keep her comfortable, of course. There's a very good palliative care unit here in the hospital that you should consider."

"My father also had a stroke. My mom wanted to give him every chance to live, every chance. We were prepared to give him full-time care." Lea held her breath as she lied again, her gaze fixed on the flooring—institutional speckle to hide the dirt. The family conference room was a mere hallway away from her mother's ward. Already, she couldn't remember the shape of her mom's nails or the pattern of freckles on her nose. "You should be doing more for her," she said, surprised at her accusatory tone.

THE NEXT DOCTOR WAS KIND. Unrushed. In vinyl-covered chairs, he sat knee to knee with Lea and went over every test, explaining its purpose and result. He offered up chances in low percentages.

He inquired about Lea's family, whether she had siblings, whether her mother had siblings. He asked how Lea's dad had died and about the quality of his death. When he asked what her parents had valued in their lives and whether they had spiritual beliefs, she stood and excused herself, claiming an urgent need to visit the washroom.

Later, when Lea talked about her mother's death, she always said, "I lied to the doctors. I told them Mom would want every opportunity to live. So they put in tubes—an NG, a catheter, an IV. She didn't look like she was in pain, but I never asked if she might be."

And kind friends usually asked, "How long was it before she died?"

"A few weeks. Terrible weeks. But you know that bird I told you about? I went back into the green bin, unwrapped the newspaper, and pulled out a tail feather." It had taken some strength. Her stomach still burned in disgust.

"The creature was dead, Lea. It couldn't feel anything. What does it matter?"

Others couldn't see how it mattered, but Lea knew. Knew that if she reached inside her purse, there'd still be an empty white envelope.

# Force Field

If I think about what I'm doing, I'll never get off the plane. After all, it's ridiculous to believe a computer algorithm can predict two strangers will develop a meaningful relationship. It's even more ridiculous to test that prediction by flying halfway across the country after a few dozen hours on Zoom. And to Saskatchewan, no less, the one province I've never visited, never even had any interest in visiting. It's possible I've spent a lifetime looking for love in all the wrong places. But it's also possible I should abort this madness—take the first flight back home. I mean WTF?

But there he is, and here I am, in the arrivals area at the Regina airport. The space between us quivers, as if some superheated prairie air hovers there, a force field I must pass through. I push aside all the expectations and disappointments of my thirty years and straighten my spine, reminding myself that it's curiosity, not desperation, that has brought me here. Still, it says something about my confidence that in the back of my mind I'm thinking stock auctions and cows on display, the knowing eye of the farmer appraising girth, teats, the capacity to breed.

"Margaret?" My own pseudo-scientifically selected farmer has a bouquet of flowers in hand and more than a little doubt in his voice. "Margaret Dean?"

"Yes, it's me, Maggie Dean." I put down my pack and we share an awkward hug. "It's good to finally meet you in person, Wyatt."

We release and he holds me at arm's length, as if our first hug has unnerved him somehow. I wonder if it was too much a city familiarity or whether I've disappointed him already—by breasts too large or too squishy. Back home, where jeans are tight, a surreptitious look down might have given me a hint, but here, jeans are loose, the package hidden. My own response is mixed. He's a good-looking man and I'm feeling something. But it's curdled with embarrassment and wrapped up in angst. I'm reminded of the drive to Pearson airport, my best friend asking, "Why are you doing this?" and me trying to explain. "When he talks to me, I feel desired." At the terminal, Beth dropped my pack on the sidewalk and hugged me hard. "Honey, what you're really feeling is deranged."

Wyatt hands me the flowers and checks my expression to see that I understand the frivolity. We are on our way to a park in the southwest corner of the province to camp; the flowers will certainly wither en route. But it's the thought that counts. "Welcome to Regina," he says, scooping up my pack and gesturing toward the exit. Online he said he wasn't one for idle chatter and, in person, it's clear that he's not. I mentally give him a tick mark for being honest and wonder if I've got one yet in his book. For packing light, as he'd advised. Or for not making the predictable raw joke about what rhymes with Regina.

He walks half a step behind so I don't get to check him out until we're in the parking lot, loading my gear into the back of his truck. By then, he's had a good look at my ass. He's taller than I expected and narrower at the waist and hips. The computer screen had flattened his facial features, but they are pleasantly angular, his cheeks clean-shaven, his hair shiny black. His skin is darker than it appeared online, but mine might be too. It's been a sun-filled summer in the east.

"All set?" he asks when we're settled in the cab. I buckle up and nod. I'm aware that what I'm doing breaks every rule I've been taught as a woman. But I feel no edge of doubt. I've scrutinized the letters from Wyatt's ex-commanding officer and a pastor (not his, he pointed out)—both glowing recommendations mailed to me at Wyatt's instigation before he would let me agree to come. "All set," I say, as he turns the key in the ignition and we head out on the road.

IT'S NOT THAT I've never driven in a truck or seen an alien landscape or taken a risk. I've made my living by writing for organizations that require this of me—NGOs with projects in Sudan and Afghanistan and Laos. But I never expected to feel so disconnected from a part of my own country. For an Ontario girl, the lack of trees is disconcerting—unsurprising in an African desert, but just plain weird in the country I call home. And the old adage is true: pictures of the prairies don't do them justice. Nothing prepares you for that dome of sky, that endless expanse of farmland. You have to drive through it.

Wyatt lets me take it in, his eyes on the road. There is no GPS in the truck, but he hands me a folded map so I can follow our route. West on the Trans-Canada to Swift Current, south from there to a big, green-coloured block that signals Grasslands National Park. The towns around it are mere dots—pinhead communities. Val Marie, Orkney, Bracken, and, dear God, a place called Climax.

I chuckle. He chuckles. He knows what I've seen. "There's another town called Love," he says, "but they're hours apart."

"And so they should be," I answer and we both laugh. It's a good sign and the ice is broken. "It'll be near dark when we get there," he says. "Help yourself to coffee in the thermos, water in the bottles."

Wyatt gets two more tick marks for thoughtfulness and competency. I settle in to the upholstery. Usually, when I have a driver, I'm being paid to be curious. What's that? Please explain. But on this trip, I can observe without comment. I don't need to verify the facts. I've described the freedom I'm looking for in an email to Wyatt—explained that, as a writer, what I crave is a still place where my mind can wander. "I don't know, Maggie," he tapped out in response. "The prairies may be just a little too still for your liking. There's a thin line between an empty mind and a crazy one."

Lonely and reticent he may be, but Wyatt is not a man to mince words when it counts. Perhaps more than a test of our compatibility, this trip is a test of my mettle, my prairie readiness. If there's any real chemistry between us, we've already acknowledged that I'm the one who'd have to move here.

"I drove down to New York City recently," I say. "The highways were littered with dead animals. Not just the occasional raccoon, but a veritable slaughter of hares and deer." The tire debris on the shoulder of the Trans-Canada reminds me of this, hunks of rubber that look like shredded carcasses, crows standing by. "But I haven't seen one dead animal since Regina. Why is that?" I could stay silent—it's comfortable enough—but I ask the question. Old habits die hard.

"They get cleaned up pretty quick," he answers. "I was a roadkill collector once. But I got a promotion. Now I slaughter cattle."

"You're kidding?" I glance over to see if he's pulling my leg. I can't tell. He flashes me a small smile, but I still can't tell.

The highway's divided, no oncoming traffic. It's easy driving despite the eighteen-wheelers speeding by. "Can you pull over at that rest area ahead?" I ask. The acid-yellow fields of canola have been broken up suddenly by an expanse of purple-blue flowers. It's beautiful, and I want to take a picture.

"It's not lavender," I say, as Wyatt and I lean against the truck, and I pass him an open bottle of water. "Some kind of pulse, is it?"

Wyatt looks as if he's deciding something before he takes a mouthful. Had we kissed, we'd have exchanged as many germs. "It's flax," he says, stretching out the muscles in his shoulders so that the tendons in his arms pop. Flax, he says, but my ears hear a different word.

Our cards are mostly on the table. We're both looking for something to last. But, as Wyatt says, it's a rare woman "from away" who can stand the life he's offering. "I don't need another local farm girl," he's emailed. "If I want the jam made, I can hire help. What I do need is someone to talk to who can keep her dark side at bay in midwinter. A woman who has reason to travel for work and come back eager—well, that might be the ticket."

We're heading south now, toward the American border and the park. The road is rough in spots, the going slower. Where the gravel crosses a track to no visible destination, a chapel sits, its front door padlocked, its white paint peeled back to reveal flecks of black beneath.

"God with a capital G, or gods?" I ask. After all, we're here to explore the subjects that can't be dealt with at a distance: religion, family, enthusiasm toward the use of tongue.

"My mother would kill me to hear it, but I actually believe in the Furies. Once you've experienced a lightning storm out here, you'll believe it too. Horses throw themselves against the stable doors and dogs chew their ankles raw. No sane God would conjure that." He reaches across the width of the cab, squeezes my hand, lets it go. His palms are calloused. I wonder if I'm meant to feel the possibility of rough times. "But mostly I believe in Fate," he adds, "and today I believe she's kind."

THIRTY MINUTES LATER, as we near the park boundary, the sky pinks up. The truck rumbles over a cattle guard and then another.

"Let's stop a minute," Wyatt says, pulling up alongside a fenced field. In the far distance, a combine plies a long row, leaving straw in tidy piles to be baled later. I measure the number of rows, the distance the farmer has covered since daybreak, the distance yet to be covered. It must be boring work, that zigzag to infinity.

Wyatt hands me a metal tiffin box, its compartments filled with basmati rice and lentil curry, still warm, aromatic. Fresh naan spills from the bottom compartment when I unscrew it awkwardly. We sit on the fence's top rail.

"Good," I say, tipping curry onto rice, scooping both up with the soft bread. "What do you suppose he thinks about out there all day?" I ask, gesturing at the farmer.

"I don't know about him, but I listen to podcasts—lectures and fiction that I download to my phone. I need to be able to have the stuff for a conversation at the end of the day."

"A conversation with whom?" I ask.

"Well, Maggie," he says, tipping back his grubby Stetson and taking his first close look at my face before he winks. "There's the rub, eh?"

THE CAMPSITES ARE WITHIN a fenced paddock. I'm not insensitive to the irony of this, sing the lyrics to Cole Porter's "Don't Fence Me In" under my breath as a joke. But when I get out of the truck, the sheer scale of the place makes my stomach drop. It's like the hollowness of rejection, the ache of loneliness. Sure, there's a bit of topography—some undulations in the distance halfway to the horizon—but I'd hardly call them hills.

"Shit," I say, "there's really nothing out here at all. Is this what it's like where you live?"

"Not far off."

"But there are towns, other farms within sight, right?" I think of the town names in tiny print on the map. Love and Climax. He looks at me blankly. Wrong. I've got it wrong.

"There are a couple prairie dog colonies in the park," Wyatt says. "If we're lucky, we might see one tomorrow when we hike. It might surprise you to know that those hillocks, or knobs as they're known out here, are closer than they appear. If you walk for an hour and look back at this campsite, you'll have covered more ground than you expected."

I suspect he is giving me something to look forward to in the vast emptiness. There is not so much as an electrical line in sight, and prairie dogs are comical. I think Wyatt's trying for a conversation that hides his initial disappointment in my reaction. Did he hope I'd love it right away? Not realize it's the kind of place that has to grow on you? A person has to be given a reason to embrace all this. Hereditary roots, the hope of profit, true love. I don't know what holds Wyatt here. I have yet to figure out his inner landscape.

"And I should mention the rattlesnakes," he adds. I glance down at my sandaled feet, my shorts—silly choices made to bare more for him. He wears cowboy boots and jeans cut with room to spare. There is purpose to everything here, I'm finding. Words and actions—all intrinsic to long-term survival. I wonder if I can do this, both wanting to and scared to at the same time.

The evening is warm. He has unbuttoned his shirt. He pulls stuff sacks from the truck. Two tents, I notice. "Wyatt?"

His answer is quiet. "I didn't want to presume." He sets up the tents efficiently, hammers in pegs to tighten the flies. "Join me," he says when he's done, and we stretch out side by side on the top of the picnic table. There's just enough space that our bodies don't touch. We're like two figures on a sarcophagus, arms delicately crossed to protect our hearts, but in the faded light, my skin appears like white marble, his tends toward jet.

He reaches over, touches me gently. "Does the difference matter?" he asks, and I'm pleased that our minds have melded, that there is some connection between us. I straighten my arm between us and so does he. "I was born here," he adds, "but my dad came from India. The prairies killed him eventually, but I'm bred to it. It's who I am."

"If it had mattered, cowboy, I wouldn't have come this far. In the city, remember, I'm in the minority. Most people come from somewhere else."

He presses his shoulder against mine. It's dry heat on the prairies. The advantage is no sweaty palms, although he must feel my goosebumps. "Oh, give me land, lots of land under starry skies above," Wyatt sings in a sweet, melodic tenor. It takes all my self-control not to jump him and I wonder how to segue to the next moment, to tell him that I'm willing to try living in empty space but that I need something to hold on to. I can do without talk, but I do need touch.

"It's late for you," he says, when he's finished singing. "Maybe it's time to turn in." He squeezes my hand but there's no hug, no goodnight kiss. Just, "See you in the morning, sweet Maggie Dean."

I LEAVE THE TENT FLY OPEN so I can see what's outside. My sleeping bag is light, but I unzip it so that my arms are free, my legs are open, and air cools my Regina. I'm wound up tight, horny as an eighteen-year-old.

Is it some cultural residual—no sex before marriage? Or do I not attract him, now that I'm here? I am waxed and plucked, clipped and creamed. I have never been accused of being cold or prudish. My single status until now has been my own choice. But Wyatt's holding back. What gives?

Sleep is elusive, then restless. Even the silence here is different. It's like listening from inside a vacuum. When I wake in the middle of the night to the rhythmic sound of soft fist against pelvis, I feel broken. His tent is only a few feet from mine and yet this is the pleasure he's chosen? Peering out through the fine mesh, I wonder where else in the world I can turn from here. A near-full moon lights up the grasslands. It gives them an eerie, spectral quality, and I think I finally understand the scope of the hurdle between us. It's this landscape. It's not just about getting used to it. It's not for everyone. He knows that. It's not nothing.

I'M UP BEFORE HE IS. My internal clock is two hours ahead and the birds wake early. Quietly, I rifle through his gear until I come across the stove and matches. I know my way around a campsite too, and may surprise him yet. I busy myself with making coffee, and the smell of it entices him from his tent.

"Good morning," I say. "How about a kiss?" And although his eyes widen a moment, and I can hear him swallow, he leans in.

His lips are dry, the way I like them, and I want our kiss to be long and explorative, but I make it short. I draw his ass in with my hands, but then I pull back to ask, "What's for breakfast?"

It takes him a few minutes to regain his composure. We eat our oatmeal and pack up our tents, taking surreptitious glances at one another and talking only about practical things, like who will carry which gear and the weight of each of our packs. Our second night together will be spent outside the paddock. Wyatt shoulders most of the load and leads us out the gate.

What Wyatt does not appreciate is that my career has taught me to pay close attention. The mule deer paths, the mixed grasses, and the smell of sage bushes are not lost on me.

"Watch out," I say, and he suspends his foot in the air. "Not a snake," I tell him. "Look." A dark songbird, rising from the ground, has left behind a half-hidden nest, two tender eggs. "Her attempts at distraction gave it away," I add, pushing the light cover of wheatgrass back into place, helping to keep her secret.

It's easy walking. No bugs. No roots or branches. Small, dried flowers rattle and crunch underfoot. I begin to distinguish shades of brown and sand colour, tuck pebbles in my pocket as if exploring on the beach. My mind is wandering, my thoughts expansive, and I trust Wyatt fully not to get us lost.

He turns then. "You go ahead for a while," he says. "Just aim for that height of land, okay?"

"Okay," I say, making sure we touch as I brush by him. I've rolled up my shorts as high as they'll go. From behind and below, my legs will appear longer. The top of the rise is as good a place as any to make another move. I run for it, feeling bold, even playful.

I don't expect what happens next. "Wy-att," I call out.

He must hear the fear in my voice.

The bison is just below us, had been out of our sight as we'd approached the rise. It is a huge and hairy dark splotch on the tan-coloured landscape, and I can tell it's pissed off at the disruption. Its tail points high, its horns hang low, its hooves rake the loose soil.

Wyatt draws me back, pushes me flat to the ground. "Stay down," he says, his body covering mine as he inches us backward over rocks and small cacti that scrape and sting my skin. I sense the animal taking a step toward us—it vibrates through the ground—and wriggle back faster, thinking shorts are stupid; I should have worn jeans.

We don't move for ages, but I don't know how long for sure. When Wyatt lifts his arm from where it has lain protectively across my neck, I turn and kiss the fabric of his shirt. "It's moved off," he says.

"You didn't think to mention the bison?" I say, despite taking in the fenced-in campsite, the patties in the fields.

He bobs his head left and right. "I didn't want to scare you off completely."

I flip onto my back. He runs his hands up my legs, brushing off the dirt, the small pebbles that have pressed into my bare flesh. When his fingers reach my inner thighs, I grip hard with my muscles like a vise.

"Here? Now?" he asks, but I know he wants to.

I release his fingers and he lays them on my arm. "What I love about this place," I say, "is that there is absolutely no one within a hundred miles who can see us."

I roll on top, press his ass and shoulders into the rocks. "Come on, Wyatt, I need to get a better sense of what I'd be committing to here."

His eyes are closed, his pelvis arching up to meet mine. We've found an oasis in this boundless place. But Wyatt is ever practical, even as he grips me. "Maggie," he says, "you really need to see this place in winter first."

Of course, it will be cold. The grassland's secrets will be covered in snow. But we're two now, so it can't get any lonelier. I'll book my flight.

He kisses me.

It will be stark in winter, to be sure. I imagine something that feels open and endless. Lying here, doing this, I don't have a problem with that.

# Relative Grief

I open the door after the third staccato buzz. With a waft of mothballs, dust, and horse manure, Edna steps too close to me. It makes me squirm, but I resist stepping back. At eighty, Edna has avoided cancer, arthritis, diabetes, and heart disease but suffers sight loss from advanced glaucoma. She peers into my face from six inches away as she kicks off her rubber boots. Clods of mud hit my wall.

"Anna?" Her voice is rough and querulous.

"No Edna, it's Alexa," I reply.

"I knew that," she blusters and pushes past me into the hall. I take her overnight bag. It's the first time I've seen my mother-in-law since Jackson's funeral. His clear blue eyes and square jaw hide in her brittle skin. I'd forgotten the resemblance, hadn't prepared myself to be slammed by the memory. I've made it through a year and all the milestones of grief that a year can bring, but suddenly I want to keen again.

It takes effort to swallow, to reassert myself against the rising tide of throat-tightening longing for those eyes. That jaw. The sound of my unwilling saliva as it is pushed down my throat is so loud that I'm sure even Edna hears it. "I'll take your coat," I finally say, and we play a gentle tug-of-war before Edna lets it go. Her eyes dart about as if looking for something. "I'll just hang it here on the newel post, so you know where it is." Her expression dares me to reach for her handbag. She clutches it to her belly.

Edna doesn't ask how I am. She has the country tendency toward breviloquence. The upside is that she doesn't intrude on my life here in the city. We've talked three, maybe four times since Jackson died.

"When's your appointment?" I try to sound interested.

"Tomorrow at eight. I'll take a cab to the station after. I'll be out of your..." She searches visibly for the next word. House? Hair? I don't prompt her, so the sentence is left hanging.

"I can take you to the station."

"Nonsense," she answers, as her lips roll inward and disappear.

I position myself on the sofa and pat the seat cushion next to me to provide an audible clue. "Shall we sit?"

She sits. A pouter pigeon barely perched.

I watch the dust motes and try not to mark the silence with measures of time: finger taps, knee bounces, or sighs.

Then Edna announces, loud and belligerent, "I used to live here, you know. I kept a nice house. The kids never had to be ashamed to invite a friend over."

She didn't live here. Ever. Jackson and I purchased the townhouse new. Open concept, with pot lights and a linear gas fireplace, it could never be mistaken for something other than a modern build.

I try to keep my tone gentle. "Do you mean that Jackson used to live here?"

"No." The word comes out on a puff of impatience. "I know what I'm saying. I used to own this house."

My gaze flits around the room as I search for explanations. I am a bird that has lost the migratory route. Can't recognize the landmarks. "You might be a little confused, Edna. It looks like your house because you used to own some of the furniture. Remember? You gave the furniture to Jackson and me as a gift." The dining room set, the sofa and settee are all antiques that Edna collected at farm sales and crowded into her East River home until Jackson and I married. Our marriage was an excuse for her to cull the bigger bits and send them to the city in a cousin's truck. Jackson and I promised each other we'd use them for five years, but no more.

Edna tries but fails to rise from the couch. "I'm not confused at all! This was my house!"

I stall. Or acquiesce. "Sorry. I didn't know." I hate my tone. It's the same one I cultivated for Jackson. *It will be all right, my love. You'll be fine.*

I can't think of anything else to say. I wait some moments. "I'll make us some tea." I leave her on the sofa. Her scrawny legs, in thick support hose, do not touch the floor. It's the first time she's ever looked frail to me. On my few visits to East River with Jackson, she'd made me think of a fighting cock. Feisty. Fierce. She'd be the first one to step up if something needed to be done. Shovel snow off a roof. Trap a fox in the henhouse. Jackson and I would track her down patrolling the country roads for signs of illegal trespassing and hunting. She'd scoff at the word activist, but everyone in the township knew her name.

I take my time with the tea, filling the kettle with more water than is needed so it will take longer to boil. I retrieve a teapot and proper English cups and saucers from the hutch instead of using the thick kitchen mugs. I pour milk into a china jug with a pattern of yellow roses that needs a rinse first to remove the dust, and then scoop loose Earl Grey into an old-fashioned tea infuser. Inhaling like an asthmatic, I fill my lungs with the fragrance of bergamot, hoping it will act like Ventolin and free my tight chest.

I am not responsible for Edna. She's Jackson's mother, I tell myself. And Anna's mother. She's not really anything to me anymore. This visit is due to mere convenience of location: the hospital to the townhouse. Nothing more.

"When was the last time Anna was up to East River?" I ask, as I place the tea tray on the low glass-topped table in front of the sofa. Edna peers at the tray. Her hand hovers above the steam but she hesitates. I pick up the saucer and nudge the cup handle into her hand.

"Who's Anna?"

I scream inside, Not fair, God! Don't put this on me! I cannot deal with another person who is incapable, insensible, incapacitated... all the words used to describe my critically injured husband until life support was removed. Until I removed his life support. Insuperably wounded, the pompous doctor had said. Anna and Edna didn't want to know what insuperably meant; from then on, they left the decisions to me.

"Who's Anna?" Edna is insistent and pokes me in the arm so sharply that it will leave a bruise. Her voice pitches higher and the vein at her temple visibly throbs.

I stare at that vein, avoiding her eyes, which are the colour of glacial runoff. The same colour as Jackson's eyes.

"Stupid country boy," Edna had said when he died. "Who the hell did he think he was, skiing in them backcountry mountains?" Her comment had shocked me then, not because it seemed unfeeling for a mother, but because I'd never heard her say *them* anything. She'd prided herself on being an educated woman and on sending Jackson to university. It was as if, with his death, she'd lost that proud part of herself.

"Anna. Your daughter."

The phone is at my left elbow. I could pick it up, excuse myself, and covertly phone Anna to tell her to come and see for herself what's going on with Edna. But I know Anna would make excuses about how hard it is to find a last-minute babysitter. We had hardly got to know each other in the two years that Jackson and I had been married; we had little but Jackson in common. Since the funeral, Anna hasn't been to the townhouse either. She calls, but our conversations rub at the scabs of our healing and leave us both raw. I expect it's been the same between mother and daughter.

Instead I get up from the sofa and retrieve a photo from the top of the hutch. I hand it to Edna. "Jackson and Anna," I say.

The photo is an eight by ten of twin brother and sister. It was taken just a month before the accident, a three-quarter shot of the two of them with their arms around each other, looking into each other's faces, laughing. Anna's long chestnut hair is caught in the breeze and the sunlight and it glows. Jackson has a five o'clock shadow that makes him look rugged and adventurous.

His left arm is around Anna's waist so that his wedding ring is hidden. Their sweaters, chosen independently, are both shades of red. They look like they could be a couple.

I hate this photo. It should be me standing with Jackson. It should be me who makes him laugh and makes his chin dimple. But it was the last photo taken before he died, and so I forced myself to frame it and prop it on the hutch. I sent a framed copy to Anna in the mail that she never acknowledged.

Edna is stiff, the photo in one hand and her empty teacup in the other.

"Are you finished?" I ask, and she pulls the photo in closer to her body as if to protect it. "With your tea?" I take hold of the saucer and wait until she releases the cup so that I can put them back on the tray.

Edna taps her finger on the glass where Jackson's heart would be. She strokes Anna's lustrous hair.

"I'm losing it," she says. Her voice is flat and hollow, low notes on the bassoon.

"Me too," I reply, rubbing my forehead as an excuse to cover my eyes. "I can't remember the way he sounded anymore. I can't remember what brand of shaving cream he used. I can't remember the shape of his feet or if his big toe was longer than the next one or not."

"It was longer." She is absolutely clear about this. "Anna?"

I don't know if she is talking to me or asking about my sister-in-law. "I'll call and see if Anna can meet you at the hospital tomorrow morning for your appointment. I can take the kids for her. I'll take a day off work."

"I mean it. I need..." Edna's jaw begins to quiver. Her thin lips curl in and all the little muscles around her nose and eyes—someone told me there are twenty-six of them—tighten. Life has carved out her face. It's Jackson's face, if we'd grown old together.

"I know," I say.

Edna's hair has lost its steel grey and has turned into wisps of white, fine as cobwebs. The skin on her face and arms seems to drip off her like candle wax. She has changed dramatically in the last year.

"Edna, what's wrong with your arm?" Her sleeve has been pushed up. There is a three-inch raw sore on the underside of her forearm. It oozes a little, as if freshly inflicted. It should be covered with gauze.

"It's nothing." She pulls her arm against herself. "It's just a little burn."

I try to be calm, looking at the striations. "Did you forget to turn the burner off on the stove? Did you burn yourself on the stove?"

She purses her lips, doesn't look at me, but nods. A moment passes.

"Let's have a drink. I think it's late enough that a drink is in order." I take Edna's elbow, help her stand and steer her to the kitchen. I pat one of the two black leather-backed bar stools on one side of the granite island. She climbs up. She still has the photo and places it carefully on the countertop in front of her like a talisman. A ground to reality.

There is only one martini glass in the cupboard. I smashed the other one, the one Jackson always used, the week after his funeral.

I'll use a goblet for myself. I splash some gin into Edna's glass and slide the bottle and the vermouth to her side of the island.

"Help yourself. I'll be back in a minute."

The stairs to the second floor seem steeper than usual. I pull on the banister to heave myself up. Off the landing, the doors to the two bedrooms are open. I turn into the master bedroom and sit on the bed.

The room is pristine. There are no clothes on the floor, no books on the bedside table. The walls, a pale grey colour that Jackson and I once thought made the room feel spa-like and serene, now seem institutional and cold. I'm sure that if I spoke aloud, the room would echo or open up and swallow the words whole.

I get up and walk across the gleaming hardwood to the spare room. I'd worried about installing the expensive polished boards when the townhouse was built. "It will get wrecked when we have a kid," I'd said to Jackson. He'd laughed and said, "Then it will look lived in, like a home. Floors should see generations..."

The spare bedroom is ready for Edna, with the big-faced clock I bought at the MedAssist store and the framed photos of East River barns. There are clean towels in the ensuite bathroom and fresh water in a jug on the night table. The furniture here, too, will be familiar to her from the East River auctions, the crocheted spread another of her homely gifts. For the last six months, I have slept in this room, felt the bits and pieces of Jackson's past graft to me, felt their roots become my own. As soon as the tears begin to burn my eyes, I swing from the room and head back down to the kitchen.

The gin bottle is blue and square and visibly emptier. I have memorized the etchings on the side: angelica root from Saxony, coriander root from Morocco, cassia bark from Indochina. Edna becomes aware of my presence. She pulls my wine glass toward her, lifts the bottle, and pours heavily. Some liquid lands in the glass; most splashes onto the counter and her wrist. The room fills with the strong medicinal vapour. It's heady, reminiscent of both ICUs and newlywed companionship.

Edna's face collapses.

I have never seen a cassia tree. I suspect that people who collect the bark choose one branch over another as much by instinct as by expertise.

"You're not going to waste that expensive gin now, are you?" I ask.

Edna catches the comic note in my voice. I am trying for something light that will complement her deeper tones.

"Well, if you insist."

She is once again the fiery lady, the proud mother. With a glint in her beautiful blue eyes, she straightens her backbone, leans her head down to the polished granite, and licks up the spilled gin with delicate flicks of her pink tongue.

She can't see my faint smile. She asks: "What are you going to do, Anna?"

I adjust the photo so that Anna and Jackson sit like two more guests at the bar. Maybe Edna and I both need company.

"Why don't you stay for a while?" I say. "Live here in the old place."

Edna says nothing. I don't know what else I expected.

# The Bus Stops Here

A blast of cold air woke me. Two dark shadows hovered just inside the flap. The beam of a headlamp swept around the floor and stopped at my feet.

"Excuse me. This is *my* tepee," I said, trying for authority.

"Plenty of room," said the closer shadow. A young man's voice, accented. "Sorry to wake you. We won't take a minute to get settled." Already the two were pulling sleeping bags from their packs. I sat up, trying to see the second person better. Was it another guy? Was this something to worry about or to take in stride—part of backpacking culture? The girl at the desk hadn't said the tepees were private, and I hadn't thought to ask.

"I'm Wolfe. This is Tyler. Don't worry. We'll stay on this side of the stove."

They didn't bother with sleeping pads. The headlight was extinguished in less than a minute. The two didn't even say goodnight to each other.

I turned away awkwardly in the narrow confines of my mummy bag, suddenly conscious of the noise its slippery fibres made against the inflated pad. The night was very quiet. I tried to stay alert to any movement from the other side of the pot-bellied stove, but my body still vibrated as if the motion of the bus was propelling it forward. Despite hours of sleep on the road, I was exhausted.

Hoping to sound confident, I said, "Well, don't..." but stopped myself. I had nothing to admonish. It was just a bad habit.

"You sure you can't hang on 'til the coast?" the bus driver had asked me a few hours earlier. "Really, the mountains, the water, they'll make you feel better."

I'd shook my head. Had to get off the damned bus. I couldn't face a third night cooped up with my misery. I'd been okay until the foothills, but their long shadows triggered something I hadn't expected.

"Thanks for stopping. I'll be okay now. Sorry about..." I nodded my head toward the bus. "... In there."

"See it all the time," the driver answered, and I'd wanted to believe him. With soft, beefy hands, he handed me my backpack and slammed the storage door with a well-practised push. "If you walk down this road about two kilometres, you'll come to a sign for a resort," he said. "It's run by some First Nations folk. They'll rent you a tepee for the night for twenty bucks."

Two kilometres didn't sound bad after nearly two and a half days on a bus. I stared down the twilit highway and shouldered the pack. Eyes peered at me through the bus's tinted windows, hostile now that I was on the outside. This was not a scheduled stop, and the remaining riders could possibly get the driver in trouble, but I figured that, overall, they'd be happy the hysterical woman was gone.

The driver gave me a fatherly look, half encouragement, half concern. "I've got to get a move on, dearie. Good luck," he said, leaving me with the impression he'd seen a bunch of young women like me and knew that luck was not all we needed. He closed the door and drove away, and I was alone on the road.

There was nothing but scrub pine forests on both sides and an ink wash of foothills in the distance, blue-grey and less distinct in the evening light. I scuffed along the unpaved shoulder in my new Teva sandals, watching their black plastic turn to grey and feeling fine grit settle between my toes. The sign for the resort lodge, when it finally appeared, was an upright pole that I might have missed except that, just as I arrived, a van turned into the driveway.

Ten minutes later, I stuffed a handwritten receipt for twenty dollars in my pocket and walked down a path, five tepees glowing white in a field of weeds ahead of me. The field was the size of a soccer pitch, but the tepees were crowded together in a circle next to the parking lot. As if by reflex, I started a plan in my head to increase the resort's attractiveness by moving the tepees to a more secluded, natural part of the property. Then I congratulated myself for this entrepreneurial instinct. At least finishing a business degree had turned out to be the right decision.

I stepped softly as I approached, hoping to avoid any encounters with other tepee dwellers, but I was immediately confronted with a dilemma: all the flaps were closed. I had no idea which tepees were occupied. Plastic flip-flops were lined up outside two—that narrowed it down. But the other three offered no clues. I listened, but the low hum of a generator outside a nearby outbuilding blocked out any smaller sounds. I loathed the thought of calling out this late at night or opening a flap to an occupied tent. What if the people inside were sleeping or making out? I'd have stood there forever, wallowing in memories of my now defunct sex life, if a blast of wind hadn't reminded me of the dropping temperatures. Slowly, one inch at a time, I lifted the first flap. Empty. I tossed in my pack and ducked to follow.

Inside, whatever romantic notions I may have conjured up about sleeping in a tepee vanished. It was spacious, but the canvas, backlit by lights from the parking lot, was splotched with mould. There was nothing inside but a rusted pot-bellied stove and a dirty brown floor covering that looked like cheap stadium turf. I followed the stove's chimney pipe up. Above me, the fifteen or so poles that gave the tent shape tangled together, leaving a gap in the canvas at the top. I pushed my pack closer to the wall with my foot. Anything in the centre of the tent would get wet if it rained, and weather in this part of the country could change fast—faster even than a boyfriend could change his mind.

It took only five minutes to unroll and inflate my sleeping pad, pull my sleeping bag from its compression sack, and fold my fleece into a makeshift pillow. I considered going back to the lodge to brush my teeth. On the bus, I'd mechanically followed the others into rest stops with grimy bathrooms. Chipped porcelain and discoloured mirrors. Beside my fellow travellers, I'd tied my greasy hair back into an unflattering ponytail, applied my deodorant stick layer over layer instead of showering. At the top of my backpack was a zippered bag holding individually-wrapped face wipes, travel-sized bottles of lotion, a blister pack that held my pills. It didn't seem to matter anymore if I took one at the usual time or not.

Now, lying flat on my back in the dark, specks of mould on the tepee's white canvas like a reverse palette of the night sky above me, reality set in. No one but me would notice whether my face was washed or my rough elbows softened with lotion. No one else would share my tube of toothpaste. I was alone.

"MORNING, SUNSHINE." I rolled over to find the guys—one a tousled blonde, one dark and grim—sitting on their packs eating Froot Loops from small boxes, an open tin of milk on the tepee floor between them.

"I had no idea they still made that horrible stuff." I hadn't seen that brand of cereal since I'd visited my grandmother as a kid.

The blond, talkative one raised an eyebrow. "Got something better over there? Maybe a little coffee from Tim Hortons, all corked up in a thermos?"

I put my head back down on the fleece. I had about three cups of yesterday's coffee corked up—just barely—in my bladder.

"New at this, are you?" He eyed my pristine sleeping bag. His, by contrast, had a greasy smudge around the collar and a rip in the blue fabric the length of a knife blade. "Where're you headed?"

I shrugged and he eyed me in a way that reminded me of the Cheshire Cat in Alice. I half expected him to say that since I had no idea where I wanted to go, it didn't much matter which way I went.

"Hitching or do you have wheels?"

Another question I wasn't sure I should answer. Not dissuaded by my silence, he continued. "We're off to a local rodeo as soon as breakfast here is over. We've got room in our van. You're welcome to tag along." Almost in unison, the two licked their spoons clean and zippered the cutlery and their rolled-up sleeping bags into the top of their packs in preparation for heading outside.

Standing at the flap, the blonde one looked back at me and asked, "You coming?"

"Are you serious? I don't even know you."

"Course you do. We met last night. I'm Wolfe. This is Tyler. It's you we don't know." He raised an eyebrow, tried to imitate that old film star from *Casablanca*—a foreigner trying to sound American. "*We'd* be taking a chance on *you*, sweetheart."

"I'm Jillian. Jill," I answered, sitting up to give him a closer look. It was the accent. Right then, I hated and mistrusted every man in the whole damned universe but I had to admit, there was something compelling about a guy with a foreign accent and a sense of humour. Under the cover of blue nylon, I pinched my thigh hard to remind myself to get a grip.

"Well, Jillian-Jill, the van leaves for the rodeo in ten minutes. We'll meet you in the parking lot. Better hustle."

As soon as the flap shut, I hustled. A rodeo? I had no better plan. I had no *other* plan. It was time to start rewriting history. Getting on that bus alone three days ago may have been an impetuous response to Ryan's unanticipated dumping, but that didn't have to stop me from pretending this trip was about grit and independence.

Wolfe flicked away a cigarette when he saw me exit the lodge. For more than ten minutes I'd been stuck in front of the bathroom mirror asking myself what the fuck I was up to but getting no good or real answer. Tyler was already in the front passenger seat of the van and didn't turn around when Wolfe tossed my pack in the back.

"Is your friend really okay with me coming along?" I asked.

"Don't mind him. He's having a bad day."

"Already?" I looked at my watch. It was just after seven.

The van was old and had been modified so that there was only one seat behind the driver. The rest of the space was crammed with stuff. A beat-up canoe was lashed to the roof.

"You guys living out of the van?" I asked. There was a vague sense of organization to the contents: a box with PFDs and a bailer, another box with food, a third containing ropes, and an unzipped duffel bag filled with carabiners, slings, and other climbing equipment.

Neither answered. Wolfe steered the vehicle out of the resort and onto the highway. He drove the speed limit. Well below the speed limit, in fact.

"Is something wrong?" I asked, trying to keep my voice even as my eyes darted from one side of the road to the other.

"Nope," said Wolfe. "But it's early, and yesterday morning around this time we almost hit a deer near here. Keep your eyes peeled."

I could picture it—the collision between terrified, soft-bellied doe and metal machine. My stomach lurched. I was suddenly apprehensive. Why had I agreed to get in a vehicle with these two athletic-looking men—these virtual strangers—whose first names were all I knew of them? I had no clue why I'd been invited along or where they were taking me. We were on an empty highway, help was getting farther away every moment, and I wasn't even sure there was cell phone service. These guys could ditch my dead body in the woods and no one but the carrion birds would know. I'd been crazy to agree to this, on top of my basic predicament, which was that I was three days from home with a pack full of equipment I'd never used before, all selected by Ryan in the days before he left my bed half empty and my credit card maxed.

"Maybe this isn't such a good idea..."

Both guys turned to eye me.

"Just breathe," said Wolfe. "We'll be out of the woods in no time."

I tried to take his advice, inhaling and exhaling slowly. At the same time, I nudged the open duffel bag with my foot to see if anything among the climbing equipment could serve as a weapon.

Tyler glanced down, watching what I was doing. Then he looked away. "Did you pick up the dead man?" he asked Wolfe.

Wolfe lifted a thumb from the wheel. "Back there."

I looked from one to the other. Their heads were still, their bodies relaxed. They weren't laughing.

"Is that supposed to be some kind of joke?" I asked, as I reached down toward the bag with my hand now, ready to grab anything metal.

But Tyler's hand got there first. His eyes held mine, amused, as he rustled among the equipment and pulled out an oddly shaped metal plate with a thick wire wound around and through it. "A deadman," he said, his smile twisted, "is a piece of safety equipment." He paused. "For climbing."

"Ah, Ty, don't be a shit. There'll be enough of that later today," said Wolfe, and the two went silent.

In no time, we were out of the trees. The foothills disappeared, and we were on the prairie.

"Are you some kind of narcoleptic?" Wolfe turned to eyeball me slouched in the back seat. I'd been startled awake by a rock to the chassis and yelped a little. Ahead, flat land and an empty highway cut straight through a sea of yellow flowers. I peered out the window, looking for a clue that would help me orient myself. I felt like I'd been asleep for days, although a quick glance at my watch told me it was only eleven. The endless prairie had put me to sleep on the bus, as well. Then, too, I'd woken up disoriented and panicky.

"Canola," said Wolfe.

"It's beautiful," I admitted, although I felt unsettled by the sheer expanse of it. Not a single farmhouse or side road broke up the vibrant colour. It was as if a child had been given only blue and yellow highlighter pens to make a picture. I stretched forward to see an approaching sign planted on the verge. Designer Rocks. "Good God, I thought you said the rodeo was local. Where the hell are we?"

"A couple more minutes and we'll be there," said Wolfe. Tyler slouched lower in his seat and stared out the passenger window.

"Is one of you involved somehow?" Neither was dressed

the part. No cowboy boots, no string ties or chaps. No horse paraphernalia in the back of the van either, for that matter.

"We're going to see Ty's kid," said Wolfe. He slowed as we approached the outskirts of a town that suddenly appeared on the other side of a slight rise in the highway. He took a couple of turns through streets with closed-up shops and parking lots full of farm equipment and joined a short line of recreational vehicles waiting to pull into a field. It was already filled with RVs of every conceivable size—from pop-up vans to mobile homes. The dirt road that wound around the outskirts of this temporary village teemed with men and women in collared shirts with rolled-up sleeves, jeans, boots, and cowboy hats. The unmistakable smell of barnyard hung in the air.

"Oh," was all I could muster.

"Never been to one of these? Not even The Stampede?" Wolfe asked.

"Never," I said. "Closest I've been to something like this was Cirque du Soleil—or maybe the Ex, back in Toronto."

Tyler snarled as we pulled into a parking spot between two trucks. "It *is* a fucking circus," he said, throwing open the door and striding off the moment the van stopped.

Wolfe and I exited more slowly. "What's with him?" I asked. "Is he an animal activist or something?" As I spoke, I found myself eyeing my surroundings for a place to bolt or hide.

"No. His wife ran off with some saddle bronc champion. Changed her name from Bess to Tiffany. Took his kid with her. The three of them follow the rodeo circuit, so Ty doesn't get to see his boy much."

Now I felt sorry for the guy. I could empathize with a story like that. As we approached the entrance gate, Tyler stood waiting, hands in pockets. He was muscled and bow-legged and could have passed for a cowboy, at least to my inexpert eye.

"At least the bitch left us some free tickets." Tyler shoved two at Wolfe, ignoring me. "You go on in. I want to find Tommy."

Wolfe and I wandered the grounds, waiting for the events in the arena to start. I followed him into the stands and wished that I'd brought a hat as the sun blazed on our heads. "Back in a sec," he said, and I nodded, taken in by the riders' preparations in the chutes next to us.

He was gone almost an hour. I'd watched the parade, the bareback riding, and the bull riding by the time he came back carrying four plastic glasses of beer. He handed me two. "Long lineup," he said. "I didn't want to have to go back." He lifted a glass toward the ring as a tractor drove in to rake out the dirt. "So, what do you think?"

"I think men are crazy."

"These men in particular, or all men?" I felt his sidelong glance. "I take it there's a done-me-wrong song in your songbook." He thrust his chin forward. "Look, the mutton bustin' is about to start. This is what we came for. There's Ty."

Tyler was standing against the rail grinning, waving toward the chutes with one hand and taking cellphone pictures with the other. One of the chute doors flung open and a sheep burst out, a kid in a plaid shirt and hockey helmet lying flat against the animal's back, clutching at the woolly neck. The kid was on the ground in no time. Tyler kept waving until the fourth kid was lowered into the chute. I could hear him yelling "Go, Tom, go!" from where we were sitting. *Everybody* could hear him. Young Tom tucked the toes of his miniature cowboy boots under the sheep's belly and hung on. But the sheep was dead set on freedom, and the boy hit the dirt about two seconds after entering the ring. Helped upright by the rodeo clown, he barely gave his father a glance before he pranced off to a gate where a woman and a cowboy—the saddle bronc champion, I supposed—waited with high-fives ready.

Tyler deflated. I knew the searing sense of rejection he was feeling, the familiar burn of acid reflux and flushing skin. I held the cold plastic of the beer against my forehead, the dripping condensation mixing with my tears.

"Hey. You okay? A little too close to home? It can't be worse than Ty's story, can it?"

"About the same, except no kids involved. The guy I was living with—Ryan—we were supposed to do this backpacking trip together. It was his big plan. Finish grad school, take a couple months off before looking for work. The morning we were supposed to get on the bus to come out here, he tells me he has a job lined up that he never mentioned he'd applied for. That he's moving out of our apartment *and* has a new girlfriend. She's a model—he couldn't keep that to himself. I know I sound bitter. But to be dumped for a model? That just..." I lifted both my shoulders and held them near my ears. Words would have made me sound like a whiner.

Wolfe kept his eye on Tyler, who thumped the top rail with his fist and then turned away from the arena and stomped off.

"Took some guts to get on the bus by yourself, though." He looked at me now. "You're kind of burned."

"No kidding," I said.

"Sorry, bad choice of words. I mean you need to get out of the sun. Come on. We're done here anyway."

"Two seconds? You two drove all this way to see a kid on an irate sheep for two seconds?"

"Yeah, well, you can be sure there was some bull fighting between Ty and Bess's guy somewhere off stage already. Ty's a good guy. But he's feeling pretty bruised by this whole thing. Misses his kid. It's hard to compete with a real live cowboy in the eyes of a five-year-old."

A model. A cowboy. I guess neither of us could measure up to the allure of a celebrity partner. In a way, I'd been caught up in it too. Ryan was smart and confident and had been determined to get a job in a big brokerage firm. I'd be lying if I said I hadn't imagined myself sharing in his success, all the trappings that went with that. Ryan had mapped out our life for us—a more ambitious plan than I would have envisioned—and I'd become a follower. I'd never doubted I would have a career, but I had to admit that somewhere along the way, I'd lost my initiative and let Ryan lead. In the end he'd called me a parasite. Just thinking about it made me want to curl up like a salted leech.

"So, what do we do now?" I asked.

There was the hint of a laugh behind Wolfe's eyes. It occurred to me that the two guys could just take off without feeling like they'd left me in the lurch. They knew I could approach anyone in the parking lot for a lift. Wolfe stayed silent just long enough to make me nervous. "Ty and I are going up into the mountains," he said, pulling my pack from the back of the van and standing it on the ground.

He didn't let it go, though. "Can I have a look at what you've got in here?" he asked and, at my nod, started emptying its pockets. Everything looked gleaming and new. It all screamed rookie camper.

"Well, you're geared up okay. High-end stuff, too. You have everything but a tent. I guess one of us can bivy," Wolfe said.

I had no idea what he meant. I just wanted to hear him say I could tag along. I may have been newly self-aware about my dependency, but I wasn't bold or confident enough to change instantly.

Tyler appeared, flinging himself onto the passenger seat and slamming the door shut. As I took my seat in the back I said, "Hey, Tyler. I'm sorry about you and your kid. He was really cute."

He seemed like he was about to snap at me until he saw my face. Instead he made a wry smile. "Yeah, thanks, Lillian," he said.

"Jillian. It's Jillian."

He reached back and put a hand on my shoulder. "*Jillian.* Sorry. I've just been so messed up by all this." He gestured out the window. "It's been two years. The kid doesn't even know me anymore."

I sucked in air between clenched teeth. Tyler had been suffering for as long as I'd lived with Ryan. Now I needed to believe that those two years didn't represent a huge bite out of my life. I needed to know I could recover, see some distance into a brighter future. I sure didn't want to look like Ty two years from now—drawn and downtrodden and heartsick.

"Yeah. That's got to hurt," I said. I glanced at each of them as Wolfe steered the van out of the field. "So how long have you two known each other?" I asked.

"This guy?" Wolfe answered. "We've been climbing together for years. When I've been at the end of my rope, Ty's been there for me. And vice versa." Ty gave Wolfe a shoulder squeeze and Wolfe knuckled Ty on the upper arm.

By the way Wolfe spoke—the loyalty in his voice—I knew these two had been through some bad times together, wouldn't hurt each other for the world. They were just two guys out on the road doing their thing.

TWENTY-FOUR HOURS LATER, I found myself camped on an alpine meadow. We'd driven all evening and half the night along highways that cut through dense green forests and past looming glaciers. We'd spent the early hours dozing in the van and, by midmorning, paddled the canoe halfway down a lake while Ty muttered in the bow about being short a PFD, and I sat in the middle with my mouth open. Mountaintops surrounded us, stately, omnipresent. "Puts things in perspective, doesn't it?" Wolfe asked at some point, and I wondered if Ryan had known this when he'd planned our trip. In the end, he was the loser for missing out. My former concerns, including Ryan, now felt petty and very small.

In the afternoon, we pulled the canoe up into the brush to hide it and hauled our loaded packs up a rocky gully with just a hint of the stream that would gush downhill each spring. We batted mosquitoes and splashed icy water on our faces and finally made it to the meadow where I collapsed among the reds and yellows and oranges of Indian paintbrush. The lake below was an impossible shade of turquoise. Ty said it was the result of glacial runoff.

I'd never been so tired in my life—and so far away from wanting to sleep.

Wolfe called to where I was perched overlooking the valley. "Jill, come learn how to use this fancy cook stove of yours." Patiently, he showed me how to prepare and eat a meal from one pot, choose a tent site that wouldn't flood, make a stone windbreak, and protect my food from alpine rodents. At dark, the two guys zipped me into a bivy tent.

"We're loaning this to you, so you'd better get used to it," Tyler said. It was little more than a sleeping bag that pulled up over my head. A single plastic hoop held the fabric away from my face. The light from Ty's headlamp barely penetrated the fibres. It might have felt claustrophobic to some people, but I felt strong after the day's efforts. I could sleep alone.

"How you doing in there, Jill?" Wolfe called out as the guys settled into their tent, and I answered, in all honesty, that I was fine. I heard them take off in the middle of the night to climb the peak behind us; they said they'd be back by the next afternoon. "Don't let the marmots bite," Ty chuckled as he strode away. He sounded like a different guy from the one I'd first met, and his new, lighthearted tone made me smile in my half-sleep. I knew he was teasing me about the marmots, but I pulled my knees to my chest all the same.

Soon after first light, I leaned back against a rock next to my bivy to eat the instant oatmeal and coffee I'd made for myself on the stove. A thick white fog, the confluence of warm air and cold water, hid the lake below. It gave the impression I was airborne, above the clouds. Once the fog cleared in midmorning, a ferry plied the waters, up and down every half an hour or so, stopping at a number of jetties to let backpackers on and off. I could see the path we'd taken the day before winding along the gully, all the way down to where we'd stashed the canoe. The lake narrowed there to a width that seemed no more than a few boat lengths. I was sure that if I waved the ferry down from the gravel beach, it would pick me up and then I could choose another place to get off. From the jetties, there were dozens of paths leading in all directions.

My gaze drifted back upward. Peaks surrounded me on all sides. I'd never given the Rocky Mountains much thought as a destination before Ryan had planned our trip. Now I wished I'd been the one to pull out a map, to jab my finger on the words snaking along the Alberta border and say, "Here! We must go here."

Maybe it was the thin air, or exhilaration from completing the strenuous hike up, but I felt compelled to reload my pack. I wrote a note for the guys on a page ripped from a paperback and left it in their tent, thanking them for the loan of the bivy. I wrote that I planned to go solo overnight and would replace the oatmeal and teabags I'd taken from their stores. I said I hoped we'd all meet up again soon, either here at the campsite or at a pub in the next town. I owed each of them a beer—a jug of beer.

At the bottom of the note, I printed my cell number, not sure if it would work. But it felt like the responsible thing to do, like I'd given thought to a plan of my own.

I left the campsite and set out on the easy downhill hike, my eyes on the solid grey bulk of the mountain that I'd picked out opposite. I would cross to it on the ferryboat. I'd wend my way through the scrub forest that skirted its lower reaches, scramble alone over boulders and up scree slopes along one of the paths zigzagging out of the treeline. Above me, the sky in all directions would look like a kid had coloured it in with that same blue highlighter pen. But the puffs of cloud would look like empty thought bubbles, ready for me to fill in.

# Beyond Cure

So late in the day, only a few pairs of skis leaned against the rack. She carried her own to the clubhouse and set them against the wall, the straps of her poles looped over the tips. Long winter shadows cast by the trees greyed the snow. Dark gravel marked a trail from the car park to the door.

Steve leaned forward from where he doled out ski passes when he wasn't coaching. "Nicky!" he said, his face bright, then dimming. "I was real sorry to hear about your mom, sweetheart."

"Hey, Steve." Her voice sounded flat, although she tried for upbeat. "It's been a hard month. First my cat, then my mother."

"Your cat?" he asked, the counter creaking.

"I had to have him put down." Damn her eyes, their quick rush to tears.

Steve twisted his scraggly beard into a single dreadlock, a hairy stalactite. "That's rough," he said finally. "Was your cat old?"

"Only nine."

"And your mom?"

"Not old enough. My cat had fluid on the lungs, the vet told me. Hard to say what caused it. Cancer, maybe."

Cancer here, cancer there, cancer cancer everywhere. The words had become an earworm. Nicky shook her head in a useless attempt to banish them. There was only one other couple in the clubhouse, but she whispered anyway. "Look Steve, I know it's late, but do you think I could get out on the trails? I've been indoors for weeks, and I really need some time out."

"I dunno, Nick. It'll be dark soon."

"I've brought a headlamp. You know I know the trails here as well as you do."

Steve glanced at his watch, then at the window. The fluorescent bulbs in the ceiling hummed loudly as if revving up to face the oncoming gloom.

"I'd get in a shitload of trouble if anything happened to you. But wait five minutes. Let me close up here, then we can drive over to The Pig and Whistle and have a beer." He winked as he spoke, tipping his head in the direction of the remaining skiers.

She tapped the counter twice. She'd known she could count on him. "Thanks, Steve, a beer sounds great."

This time he glared at her. "You heard me, right? Wait."

THE LAST OF THE DAY'S SKIERS packed up, zipping gear into bags and heading for the car park. Their goodbyes carried on the crisp air, reminders of weekends not long before when Nicky had trained hard under Steve's direction instead of passing days at her mom's bedside.

"Can we give you a lift somewhere?" asked one of the girls, hovering at the door of her SUV.

Nicky pretended to brush snow from her skis. "No, I'm fine,

thanks. Just listening to the birds." The stupidity of the remark made her blush. Who listened to birds in midwinter? But just as she said it, one swooped by and landed not ten feet away. A turkey vulture, its featherless red head hunched, its eyes expectant. She was used to seeing them along the side of the highway eating roadkill, but had never been this close to one. She tugged on her collar to cover an exposed bit of skin at the back of her neck. It felt creepy to see the bird after the month she'd just had.

THE LIGHTS WENT out in the clubhouse. The door clicked shut as Steve appeared. "Ready?" he asked, gesturing that she should follow.

It wasn't dark yet and the snow seemed to hold some light, like the luminescent stars glued to the ceiling of Nicky's bedroom when she was a kid. She and Steve carried their equipment to a small grove of pines that marked the beginning of a competition-level track.

"Look, I've lost a few people in my time too," Steve said, "so I know you probably don't want to talk. Ski at your own pace and I'll follow. But we're back at the parking lot by seven, deal?"

"Deal." An hour out, an hour back—maybe thirty minutes to an hour before it got really dark. She stepped into her bindings and pushed off.

The track felt like it had been regroomed late in the day. Smooth and fast, it was the perfect place to get into a rhythm and go. On either side, the snow looked like corrugated cardboard. It reminded Nicky of the small dishes of sand that came with miniature rakes to make personal Zen gardens. She'd admired those once. Now she knew better. Life couldn't be patterned into tidy perfect rows.

She kicked and glided, her poles swinging forward to punch the crusted surface. As they released, they made a rough sound like a crow's caw. The effect was hypnotic. Her stride lengthened. As her muscles warmed, she was able to look up and around. The trees held tufts of snow in their notches like cotton batting. Now and then, a small hunk separated and fell, indenting the unspoiled white layer below.

Steve must have thought it was odd that she'd talked more about her cat's illness than her mom's short battle with cancer. The past month still had a surreal feel that was hard to talk about. She'd been unprepared for it all, but especially for the hard decisions she'd had to make about Shadow just before she'd learned of her mom's diagnosis, and before she knew anything real about death. His ashes were in her pack now, in a small urn. She'd carried them around since her mom's burial.

"We can give your cat fluids for dehydration and try an antibiotic," the vet had said, but Nicky knew it was just to buy time to say goodbye. She'd lifted Shadow from his carrier and placed him on her bed, his body lighter than the day before, his once shining grey coat now lacklustre. For two days and nights, she stretched out beside him listening to audiobooks, alternately stroking his head and offering chicken gravy from her finger. It might have been her imagination, but she was sure he was trying to tell her something important. His pupils expanded and dilated in a code she couldn't understand. She memorized the shape of those eyes as they dulled, the angle of each silver whisker as he laboured to breathe. When he dropped off the edge of the bed and crawled to the back of her closet, she knew it was time to return to the vet.

"Am I making the right decision? Would you do the same in my place?" she pleaded. The young doctor was annoyingly obtuse. She knew vets had to be like that—they were the ones who pushed the plunger, after all—but still.

She wished now that she'd let Shadow die in his own way, on his own time. In her dark closet.

She slowed to a stop. Steve was right behind her. "Did you ever put down a pet?" she asked. "Did you ever hold it while it was euthanized?"

Steve frowned before he answered. "I grew up on a farm. It was different."

Of course. The runt of the litter drowned in the rain barrel. The old nag shot behind the barn. Why did we feel so comfortable hastening the deaths of our broken animals? What gave us the arrogance, as if we knew for sure their misery felt like our own?

She slipped her pack off her shoulders, found the silver flask inside and took a slug. The brandy burned its way to her stomach, warming, numbing. She offered the flask to Steve, but he shook his head with disapproval.

A loud crack broke the silence. Sharp, close, it reverberated off the nearby trees. "Jesus, what the hell was that?" Nicky asked. "A tree exploding?"

Steve peered into the gloom ahead. "That's a myth, that trees explode. I've heard bark pop from the cold, but that was no pop. That was a gunshot."

"Gunshot? But this is private land."

She'd stated the obvious. Steve ran a glove under his nose. "Look, Nick," he said, "either this asshole's hit something and he's had his fun, or he's going to keep shooting until he's finished the job. We're targets out here in the dark."

"We have our lights."

"And we're gonna use them to get you to the warming shelter up ahead. I've got to go back to the clubhouse and report this jerk."

"I'll ski back with you."

"I don't want you to risk it. You're in a black jacket, dammit." He adjusted his own headlamp so that it flashed, talked in a loud voice the entire time they were on the move. At one point, he slowed up, casting light over the snow where the track had been disturbed. Dark splotches turned crimson in the lamplight. Droplets trailed off into the trees. "Oh, Christ," he said and put on more speed.

AFTER STEVE LEFT HER at the warming shelter, telling her he'd be back as soon as possible, Nicky assembled dry matches and newspaper to light the wood stove. When the kindling took, she added split logs—enough to create heat and provide a warm glow so she wasn't sitting in the dark. Skiing had felt good but she'd gone out hard. Now her muscles stiffened in the cold.

She squatted, extending one leg to the side and then the other until she felt the muscles burn. In the centre of the shelter, away from the door and windows, she felt safe. But it was silent and shadowy, acrid with the smell of smoke and dusty with mouse droppings. She listened for the mice, rustlings that would make her feel less alone.

From inside her pack, she lifted the plastic urn and held it in her lap. The day her mother had died, the sky had been lit with powdery sunlight. She'd stood at the window in her mother's room and tried not to yell each time one of the palliative care staff came in. "Can't you see she's still in pain? Can't you do something?"

She'd been forced to learn new vocabulary in the kingdom of the sick. The multisyllabic language of the drugs her mom had been prescribed with their hard endings—lomide and platin and istine—and the soft, obscuring words of doctors. The oncologists had moved so quickly from diagnosis—pancreatic cancer—to the futility of treatment. She was beyond curative therapeutic intervention, they'd said, Nicky slow on the translation even when the doctors suggested she gather her family for a meeting.

"But there's just Mom and me, so why do we need to meet?"

"We think it's time to discuss palliative care."

"Meaning what?" she'd asked, while her mother had answered yes, quietly, from her bed. "I'd like to be on a unit, not at home. I don't want to be a burden to Nicola." She'd articulated her goals calmly. "Conscious until the end so that I can communicate with my daughter. But I don't want to suffer."

It had been a gift of a sort, that her mom was so clear about what she wanted. It gave Nicky a role—guardian of her mother's pain control—when she felt helpless otherwise. And the staff had tried to comply, they really had. They just never got it exactly right.

"It's the one thing she asked for—the *one* thing," Nicky wailed as the nurse checked her notes and avoided meeting Nicky's eyes. Her mother groaned and shifted on the spotless bed, cried out at obstacles to her passage that Nicky could only imagine. She applied Vaseline to her mother's cracked lips with her finger, offered sips of water that eventually her mother refused.

PACING DIDN'T HELP. The warming shelter was only four strides wide. She felt like a wild creature in a pen. Steve should have been back by now. She tapped on her phone, not expecting a message. There were no bars. Already, she'd been in the shelter for forty minutes. The birds had settled for the night. Even the white pines had stopped whispering.

"Fuck this." She looked at the door, so poorly fitted that snow had blown in under it earlier in the day. It was impossible to wait. She'd never been the kind of person who could sit still for long. She packed the small urn back into her pack, recalling Steve's frown when her hand brushed against the flask again. Another slug of brandy would give her the courage she needed. Hell, she might as well finish the whole thing.

SHE FOUND THE SPOT again easily, the reddened snow. The deer had been shot on the trail itself. It must have fallen—there was a large indentation where the blood was thickest—and then scrambled upright and limped off into the forest on the trail's west side.

The hoof marks were obvious but it was hard going to follow them, the soft snow up to Nicky's knees. Cold flakes worked their way into the small gaps between her ski pants and boots, chilling her ankles. She tried to focus on her movements through the thick underbrush and not what she would do if and when she came across the deer. Or the hunter.

The animal was closer than she expected. The hunter could have found it easily, so maybe he didn't even try.

It lay on its side, flank heaving. As soon as it sensed Nicky's presence, it tried and failed to flail upright, kicking its long, thin legs around uselessly. The whites of its eyes showed. Its breath condensed in the air in steamy puffs.

Without looking away from the animal, Nicky called out, "Is anyone there?" Her words didn't reach very far, and she was ashamed of her weak volume. She rationalized that her shout had been quiet on purpose, because she didn't want to frighten the deer any further. It was young and without antlers, agitated but incapable of escape.

The wound was to its neck. Nicky made small, encouraging sounds as she approached, the kind she'd used with Shadow and—it embarrassed her now, as she realized it—her mom. The air was tangy with the odour of wet fur, blood, and ammonia. The deer had pissed where it lay.

"It's okay," she whispered, as she dropped to a crouch by its head. Its brown eyes were flecked golden, jumbo-sized marbles of fear. Nicky wanted to reach out and stroke its pelt or the small hairs on its ridiculously large ears, but she was filled with doubt. Her presence was clearly no comfort to the animal. So why was she here?

"NICOLA? SWEETHEART?"

She'd never forget how her mother's voice had sounded then, the many registers of pain within it. A spasm rippled across her mother's face, rumbled down her torso so violently that Nicky could see the thin sheet rise and fall like a wave.

"You're awake, Mom? How are you feeling right now? Is there anything I can do for you?"

"Make it stop, Nicola. I can't take it anymore."

"Do you want more medicine?"

There was surprising strength in her mom's fingers. Surprising intensity in her mom's dark eyes. "Keep squeezing my hand, Nicola. I want to go."

THE DEER RAISED ITS HEAD and struggled again, its snout hitting Nicky's knee, sending an electric pulse through the nerves of her thigh, forcing her to take a sharp intake of breath. She'd never had a severe injury. What did she really know about pain?

The turkey vulture was back. It fluttered down and stood nearby, beak hooked and cruel-looking. Nicky had no knife in her pocket. No sharp-ended stick lay nearby.

One way or the other, the deer would die. She risked putting a gloved hand on its head, now lowered, the wound facing the ground. When the deer didn't move, she sat in the snow next to it, the length of her leg along its back, and felt its warmth. For what seemed like a long time, she watched its side rise and fall, hoping the breaths would slow, that the end would come. But it continued to breathe, and she wasn't sure if it keened or she did.

SHE WOKE WITH HER CHEEK against the sheet of her mother's bed, her hand on her mother's cold, dry fingers bent around the morphine pump. She detached the one from the other and examined her mother's face, trying to read the expression. A few minutes without pain at the end may have been enough to ease the way. When she found a nurse in the hall, she said, "My mother died in my sleep."

SHE TRIED TO PICTURE the last really colourful thing she could remember seeing. The flower arrangements at her mom's funeral, maybe. She had a short, fat piece of branch that she'd clawed from beneath the snow and the lace she'd taken from her boot. She worked the lace under the deer's snout and around its ears, tying it off above, then below the neck wound where she thought she could feel a vein. Through the tree canopy above, stars glittered, more than she'd ever seen in the city, maybe more than she'd ever seen anywhere. Everything else was shades of black and grey.

The deer still breathed. She placed the stick under the knotted lace and twisted, then twisted again. It tightened and held. The deer shuddered, but weakly, not enough for Nicky to lose her grip. Maybe it was fighting severe pain or—more earthly than godly—resigned to it.

Experience, she found, had not inured her to death. There was no relationship here and she wasn't sure of her obligation. Perhaps it was to assist. Or perhaps, this time, it was merely to witness, to see the deer to the end.

She twisted the stick until the lace was tight against the deer's hide without causing any pressure. The turkey vulture made a sound like it was interrupting, clearing its throat. Farther off, Steve called out her name. The vulture was close now, its eyes greedy. Behind Nicky's own eyelids, a kaleidoscope of colours—yellow, blue, and crimson red—replaced the grey-black film of darkness. She thought of Shadow's ashes and how she might bury them with the deer. She wished she'd been a better, stronger guardian of her mother's death. There was plenty of strength in her shoulders and biceps now, if she needed it. She listened. She waited for her conscience to speak. She counted to ten.

# Housing Crisis

Amy's second reaction was to step to the left so she couldn't be seen through the kitchen window. Her third reaction was to swipe and tap on her phone until she heard it dialing Julie.

"You know it's five thirty in the morning, right?"

"There's a man in my treehouse," Amy whispered.

Julie's laugh fluttered in her ear. "Well, I haven't heard that one before, but good for you!"

"No, seriously. Maybe I didn't tell you my new place has a treehouse. Should I call the police? Tell me what to do."

Moments before, Amy had approached the kitchen window with her eyes closed, knowing that when she opened them she would experience her first sunrise in the first house she'd ever owned. She had complete faith that the colours wouldn't disappoint. Fiery red at the horizon would fade skyward to a wash of fluorescent pink and deep-ocean blue, just like in the photo that had sold her on the property. It would be perfect, one of those memories that would become secret and indelible, a celebration of a milestone in life only she would attend.

Except that what caught her eye was not the sunrise. Directly in front of her, a naked man stood on the treehouse platform, his pee arcing into the garden below.

Her first reaction—before she stopped herself—was to lean forward to rap on the glass, but what she saw reflected there was a petite woman in a nightgown. The man outside had a broad chest, thick thighs, and a huge penis. In less than a second, her disgust at his act transformed into a mental image of being overwhelmed, silenced, and violated. Calling the police was an option, but would they take her seriously? She slipped into the shadow, hoping her movement hadn't caught the man's attention. There she dialed Julie, the only person she knew who would answer her call regardless of the time.

Julie's laughter wasn't quite what Amy expected. She said she didn't think the situation was a real threat or merited calling the police. Instead, she told Amy to go back to bed. According to Julie, the guy would clear out by the time any reasonable person woke up. She couldn't seem to get over what she thought was the funniest euphemism she'd heard in a long time. "There's a man in my treehouse," she kept repeating, until Amy said she had to go.

Light was already infiltrating the kitchen by the time they hung up. There was no way Amy would be able to get back to sleep, and work didn't start until ten. She darkened her phone screen so its glow couldn't be seen through the kitchen window, then lowered herself to her knees. As she crawled past the kitchen table, she nabbed the cast iron frying pan from where she'd unpacked it the night before. Passing by the back door, she glanced at the bolt. It was horizontal, and she couldn't remember if that meant locked or unlocked.

BACK IN HER BEDROOM, Amy waited. She would give the guy until eight to clear out. With any luck, the problem would resolve itself. It would only get complicated if she had to move on to reporting her trespasser or confronting the man herself. Both had downsides. Involving the cops would take up her morning, and who knew how the man would respond if she approached him at daylight on her own. Offering him a cup of coffee and a polite but firm declaration that he please leave felt like the moral high ground, but it was still nerve-wracking. The man had heft and, being new to town, Amy had no one to call on for support. Julie was back in Vancouver, now a ninety-minute ferry ride away.

The deadline passed. Amy crept to the dining nook, which had the only other window view of the garden. There was no sign of the man. Maybe he'd gone back to sleep after relieving himself. What she could see was that his occupation of the treehouse was not impromptu. A garden hose was attached to the faucet by the back door, the nozzle hanging in a bucket by the treehouse's rope ladder. And an electric cord was strung between the outdoor outlet and one of the tiny shuttered windows that flanked the treehouse door.

So he was both a freeloader and a thief, she concluded, wondering how much water and electricity he'd consumed in the months her new house sat vacant while she finished up at her last job. The property manager she'd contracted to look in on the place regularly must have been negligent. The first thing she'd do when she got to work was call him.

SHE'D LOOKED FORWARD to a leisurely walk to work, but the distractions of the morning forced her to rush. Arriving late on her first day wouldn't set a good example. She was determined to make a good first impression as the newly appointed office coordinator of Barker and Lane Consultants. There was a mortgage to pay, higher than her previous rent and on a lower salary. Eliminating transit costs, moving to a smaller town on Vancouver Island, and accepting more limited job opportunities were concessions she'd made to afford the house.

But it was worth it, she assured herself, trying to fill with air those parts of her lungs that always felt collapsed. The corners of her mouth twitched into a smile, and she walked faster just thinking of her little bungalow, space that was all hers and completely under her control. Of all life's milestones, owning a home was the only one she'd been able to achieve. A partner, kids, a successful career, world travel—at forty, these events seemed destined to remain out of reach. But owning a house was an accomplishment that almost none of her city friends had managed. She couldn't believe how much satisfaction she'd got from the responses to her photos on Instagram. She had been a little disingenuous—posting close-ups of the burled oak fireplace surround, the established perennial gardens in front and back, and the walk-in closet without ever sharing that the total square footage was less than that of her friends' condos. That she had a yard with actual grass was enough to elicit the desired responses. *You're soooooo lucky!* and *I'm soooooo jealous* were her favourites, and she always tapped the heart icon to reinforce her self-satisfaction. For once, she understood what it was like to humblebrag on social media and experience the envy of others.

By the end of the day, Amy was stressed. Her new boss had been unable to meet her as planned and had left her in the hands of an assistant who was too busy to give her a proper tour and introduction to the other employees. Deposited at her new desk with little instruction, she spent the first hour trying to contact the property manager, who had seemed decent and responsive when she first engaged him but was suddenly unreachable by phone, no matter how many messages she left. She tried the number so often that she eventually had to escape to the women's washroom to avoid the curious glances of the people at desks around her. And the day had been more challenging than she expected. It wasn't easy to project confidence and affability without giving her new colleagues—most in their mid-twenties—the idea that she was a lightweight. Her oversharing probably didn't help, but the temptation to slip into the conversation a comment about her new house had been too great. She thought it would elicit some respect for her lengthier work experience and signal that hard work paid off, but it seemed to have the opposite effect. Maybe in smaller towns home ownership had a different significance than in the city, marking someone's stagnation or immobility. Or maybe the slim hopes for traditional markers of success had been completely quashed in the next generation.

Their glances shifted to and from their phones as she tried to break the ice, making them appear both disinterested and disdainful. It was as if they understood aspiration as something only to do with breathing.

She called Julie as she glumly trod home along weed-infested sidewalks.

"So, how was it?" Julie's voice was loud, usually a sign she'd had a drink or two. "Any more men to shake out of the trees?"

"Sorry, I'm not in the mood for jokes."

"That bad?"

"I thought I'd like being in charge of an office. I was told it was like a family, but they're all so young. It feels like they're putting in time before they make their escape. I can feel their suspicion. They're asking themselves why I left the city to come here."

"So, did you tell them you left so that you weren't still living with a roommate in your forties?"

"How's the new roomie?"

"She's not you. It sucks. I wish I could afford a place of my own."

"You could come here. Buy a place nearby."

"You know I'd die in a small town. How'd it turn out with Tarzan, by the way? Did he clear out?"

"I'll let you know once I get home. Call you later?"

"Yeah, sure. Go get him, girlfriend."

It wasn't until Amy hung up the call that the tone in Julie's voice struck her as odd. It seemed to contain a note of mockery, as if Julie didn't think Amy could deal with this problem on her own.

The backyard was fenced and, like a lot of yards in the area, it was surrounded on three sides by a cedar hedge high enough to provide a screen from the neighbours. Amy stood by the gate. The yard was private, but it was also cut off from view. A sensation like rising hackles crept up the back of her neck.

"Hey!" she called out. "Hey, you up there!" The door of the treehouse was wide open. Next to the main house, the garden hose lay coiled; the bucket and electrical cord were out of sight. She steeled herself to ascend the rope ladder, something she hadn't done when she'd toured the property initially because the real estate agent counselled her not to until a safety inspection had been completed. Later, when she'd received the report, it assured her that the little house was well built and to code and that she wouldn't have to go to the expense of removing it if she didn't want to.

She started up the ladder, happy now for shoes with heels that caught and held her to the ropes. At platform level, she realized the treehouse was bigger than she expected and that the door had been left open almost as an invitation for her to look. The man was tidy to the point of military precision. Lined up on a shelf were a two-burner camp stove, a flashlight and gooseneck lamp, a phone charger, and a rolled-up sleeping bag. Stacked milk crates displayed clean pots and metal dishes, a few tinned goods and boxed staples, and three books (the top one titled *Planting and Foraging*). A zipped suit bag hung from the ceiling, thick enough to enclose more than one change of clothes. With the exception of a couple grains of rice stuck between two planks on the floor, the place was clean. The whole set-up was snug and dry, and Amy had no trouble standing upright.

"Well, crap," she said out loud. "I'd live here too. It's practically one of those tiny houses." She caught sight of a small pair of field glasses resting on the window ledge as she turned to leave. She picked them up to assess the view. Just as she feared, her trespasser had a perfect eye on her kitchen. She could see the unpacked dishes where she'd left them on the table.

"Well, that's it, buddy. I don't care how tidy you are." Startling a flock of chittering sparrows, she shut the treehouse door behind her. In her mind, she was already crafting an eviction notice she'd tack to the base of the ladder. Looking down, she was surprised to see vegetable plants peppered throughout her perennial garden.

"WAIT A MINUTE," Julie said. "I'm putting you on speaker so I can get a glass of wine. So Tarzan has been there long enough to grow vegetables?"

"Uh-huh. Mostly tomatoes, green onions, basil. So, what do I do now?"

"Listen to yourself. You just told me you were going to print off an eviction notice. That's what you do now. Otherwise, you'll be giving up your property rights to a squatter."

"Is that a real thing?"

"Did you go through his stuff?"

"Why would I do that?"

"To see if there were drugs, stolen wallets, pictures of naked women. He's obviously a peeper."

"That's not—"

"Amy, didn't I teach you anything in all the years we lived together? If it walks like a creep and acts like a creep... Hey, did you hear back from the property guy?"

"He left a message. Said he totally understood how upset I was, and that he plans to come over to the house tomorrow evening to discuss it."

"So, it's status quo tonight? Tarzan's at home?"

"I guess he could be. I haven't looked. I have a ton of work to do for tomorrow, so I'll put my notice out for him in the morning."

"You're killing me. Do you want me to draft it for you?"

"Of course not," Amy answered. She frowned at the phone screen, wondering how and when Julie had concluded she was so incompetent and needy.

FOR THE REST of the evening, Amy worked at her desk. She left her phone in the bedroom on purpose, disappointed that she'd called Julie three times in one day. She loved her friend, but after more than thirteen years of living together, people who knew them both had started to treat them more as a couple than as longstanding roommates. She'd let years slide by until she woke up one day on the cusp of middle age with nothing but some decent savings in the bank and the reputation of being a closeted gay. And while Julie had purported to be supportive of Amy's decision to relocate to Vancouver Island, she'd also pointed out that Amy wasn't used to being independent—an observation that had rankled because of its obvious truth. Amy needed to prove to herself she could sort out problems like Tarzan on her own.

Just before bed, she fired off a text to Julie: *Going to be a crazy wk. Taking break from non-work-related media and phone.* And since there was a good chance Julie wouldn't believe her, she added: *I'll call u Saturday.*

THE FOLLOWING MORNING, it was raining so hard that there was no point tacking up a paper sign. Standing on two books to appear taller should the guy have eyes on her, Amy mustered up enough confidence to look out the kitchen window. There was no sign of the man. She stepped off the books. Allowing him to live in her treehouse was an untenable situation. Untenable, she repeated in her mind, feeling more in control just using the word. She'd learned it only recently from the Word-a-Day calendar her previous boss had given her as a going away gift.

She slogged to work in a waterproof coat and rubber boots, leaving early enough that she could change into heels before anyone else turned up. There was another message on her work phone from the property manager.

"Just confirming our appointment tonight at seven. Again, please accept our apologies for whatever damages that may have incurred. I know we can sort this out."

Perfect, she thought. She'd never mentioned any damages, but an apology was as good as an admission of guilt. She'd demand a refund, and she'd send the guy into the backyard to dislodge Tarzan. By tonight, she'd be back in charge, master of her own domain. She might even find a use for that treehouse, take up sketching or writing. She needed a hobby to fill the time she used to spend drinking wine and binge-watching Netflix with Julie.

Her second day on the job was harder than the first. It became increasingly clear that the office was dysfunctional, and she'd been hired to clean it up. Skimming through personnel files, she discovered that at least three of her staff were underperforming. Her predecessor had been doing the prep work to fire them.

She wanted to call Julie but resisted. Maybe once the treehouse issue was out of the way, she could ask Sam, the property guy, for advice on how to fire someone. He'd mentioned upon hiring that he'd been running his business for over ten years; surely, he'd have the experience she didn't. And getting rid of her trespasser was a kind of firing. She'd watch the process closely.

Sam arrived on time, ringing her doorbell just as she turned on all the lights in the house for the first time. She glanced outside. The electrical cord was, once again, strung between the outlet and the treehouse. "Gotcha," Amy said, and went to let Sam in.

She'd imagined someone middle-aged, a little soft around the edges. This man was trim and smelled of lemon and sandalwood.

He pressed a bottle of wine and a potted begonia wrapped in clear plastic into her hands. "It's Amy, right? I am so sorry. I hope these go some way to making up for what our services may have lacked."

Both her hands were now full. In the narrow hallway, she and Sam were forced to stand close together. It felt more like a date than a business meeting. She put the bottle and plant down on a hall table. "Thanks. Let me show you the problem."

He glanced into the living room, took in the floral patterns that Amy hoped didn't suggest a woman living alone. "Why don't we open that bottle of wine first?"

"Pardon?"

Sam gestured to the living room and smiled. "We've both worked today, and I'm guessing we're both tired. So why don't we talk over a glass of wine? You can explain to me exactly what the problem is."

"I guess. But follow me into the kitchen first. I'll get glasses, and you can see for yourself. Someone has been living on my property—clearly for months—and I want you to get rid of him. Our contract was for house and yard maintenance, and security. Look." She hesitated, but the only way to really see outside was to turn off the kitchen lights. She waved Sam to the window.

"What am I looking at, exactly?" he asked, leaning toward her as if to adjust his view, warmth radiating through the linen of his jacket.

She stepped aside. "It would be better if we went outside."

He followed her. She stopped at the base of the ladder. "After you." The height of the cedar hedge and the isolation of the yard began to weigh heavily. She wasn't about to let this stranger get a view of her ass by preceding him. "The guy's been tapping into my water and my electricity."

"You don't say." Ahead on the platform, Sam was directing his cellphone flashlight into the treehouse. "Wait," she said, when she joined him. "Give me that."

There was nothing. The treehouse was completely vacant. No sleeping bag, no milk crates, just the piney, mouldy odour of raw wood and neglect. Even the electrical cord that she'd seen draped through the window a few minutes earlier was now gone. Amy shone the light on the floor, bending over to get a closer view. No rice in the cracks either.

Sam blocked the door, had nudged it almost shut. Despite the dim light shrouding his features, she could sense how his attitude had changed. His expression held a feline self-satisfaction. He took up space like a man about to sweep in his winnings after a well-played hand of poker.

"Well, it looks like your little problem has been solved. I don't see any damage." He took a step toward her. "So how about we have that glass of wine now?"

Amy tried to slide by him, but he turned suddenly so that his arm brushed against her breast. "Sorry," he said, as she blurted out, "This is just so weird. I know the guy was here earlier. There was a camp stove and a bag of clothes."

"Well, the important thing is that the property is safe now."

Amy rubbed a hand along her hip. Her phone wasn't in her pocket. "Look," she said. "I'm sorry about this, but..."

Sam didn't move. Dampness spread across Amy's upper lip. She was acutely aware that today was Tuesday, that Julie wouldn't expect to hear from her again until Saturday, and that no one who reported to her would care if she turned up at the office tomorrow or not.

"Excuse me," she said again. Sam wasn't as big as Tarzan, but he had the height and bulk to overpower her. She still couldn't help thinking his expression resembled that of a cat who'd cornered a bird in a bush where it had thought itself safe. This was exactly the kind of situation she should have been smart enough to avoid. Her voice, when she finally found it, came out higher pitched than she intended. "Would you please step aside, and let me get down."

The question of what to do if he didn't move was just passing through Amy's mind when a two note, high-low whistle pierced the night. It was the kind of signal someone might use to get the attention of a pet, though as far as she knew no dogs lived nearby. The sound was followed by a wood and metal clang as her kitchen door slammed.

Sam moved immediately to let Amy pass onto the treehouse platform, and they both clambered down the ladder. Back on the ground, Amy peered into the gloom but saw no one. She strode to the side gate and opened it to indicate Sam should use it to exit. She wanted him off the property immediately. She could have pressed him for a refund but knew she'd get nowhere. She knew his type.

Back in the house, she flipped on the kitchen lights and stood at the window looking out at the shadowy outline of the treehouse. On the outside sill where she was sure to see them, a half-dozen ripe cherry tomatoes were arrayed like gifts, each topped with a green bow of tiny leaves. As she stood in silence, she searched for a figure in the blueness of the yard, but there was no movement except for the dark outlines of sparrows darting between trees and bushes. She saw her face reflected back to her, low in the window glass—a small woman alone in a small house, resisting what she knew was a ridiculous urge to call out: Come back. You can stay.

# Transient

I was born on a beach. Sometimes people don't hear me properly when I say this. They think I've said I was born a bitch and look at me weirdly until I repeat myself. But it's true. I was born on a beach, my mom out camping when my early advent caught her short. By the time the ambulance arrived, my dad had guided me onto a towel and cut the cord with his Swiss Army knife.

I have theories about birth. Children born by C-section in hospitals are rule followers, children born in water swim against the current, those born in their parents' beds focus on family. But kids born on beaches? There can't be too many of us. The sand between our toes makes us restless. Our eyes are always fixed on the horizon.

IN BED, Josh throws an arm over my midriff. The room is frowsty from sleep and last night's sex.

"Don't go," he says. "I'll miss you."

I shift, tumble his arm to the sheet, and try to keep the conversation light. "You'll live," I say. "It's only for one night. Thank your sister for the truck."

Josh makes a last snatch for my hand. "Don't you have her bachelorette tomorrow?"

"I'll be back in time," I say. "I just need to stare at the waves for a while."

He flips onto his back and wets his lips as his brow furrows. "There won't be many people camping out this time of year. Promise me you'll call when you get there."

At my nod, he smiles and leans forward to plant a long one. "Love you."

"Love you, too." I pull a hoodie over my head and use the inside fabric to wipe my mouth dry. These are new, these deep, wet kisses that leave trails of saliva between us. They make my jaw hurt. I've started grinding my teeth.

WHEN I MET JOSH IN VIETNAM, I'd been on my own for six months. We carried the exact same model of backpack.

"Hey, you must be from Canada," he said, as we both entered a guesthouse in Sapa looking for a room. We named adjacent towns on the West Coast as we waited for keys.

Four beers later, we tucked into a dinner of omelettes flecked with herbs and whatever was cooked last in the restaurant's one cast iron frying pan. I liked the way Josh's cheeks hollowed when he sucked back a Saigon Special. I liked his mala beads and the patch of duct tape that covered the hole in his boot. I thought we'd do what a lot of road warriors do: hook up for a few days before one of us split off to some other destination. But a few weeks later, instead of heading to Koh Phuket as he'd planned, Josh was still with me visiting villages along the Chinese border and scrambling in the hills. I thought, just maybe, I'd found my soulmate.

"Look," he said the night we returned to town for a shower and a real bed. "I know this is too soon and a crazy idea, but would you consider flying home with me? My mom's turning sixty, and I told my dad I'd be there for the party."

Home. At the time, the word made me stiffen involuntarily. On the road, I heard my fellow travellers talk about homesickness—the sudden aversion to the *differentness* of the place they were in—although I'd never experienced the feeling myself. I'd learned that, from a distance, some people idealize home and others think making a home "one day" is the highest calling. For me, home was the place where the people I'd grown up with—my parents, my teachers, my friends—wanted me to be exactly like them, and I felt no call to go back there. But none of this stopped me from saying yes to Josh. We'd been having such a good time having sex in exotic places—caves, row boats, the outskirts of markets. The sex was so good I'd broken my pledge to stay solo. Despite the proximity of our hometowns, I'd convinced myself Josh was the kind of person who didn't feel like the place he'd grown up was the place he was meant to stay.

In the parking lot behind Josh's apartment, I throw my pack into his sister's truck. The air has a stagnant smell from vehicles left idling too long, from nearby dumpsters, from the spray of feral cats on the tires. In the pre-dawn gloom, a familiar shape in an oversized trench coat rummages through the recycling bins for bottles.

"Hey, Mara," I call out, but not so loudly as to spook her.

Before she responds, she gives me the narrow-eyed look she gives everyone. "Do you have anything for me? I'll grant you a wish." Mara has a faint accent I can't place. Her history changes each time I ask about it.

"I put my empties in the usual place." I gesture to the bush beside the building where I found her sleeping one morning. There is now competition for returnable bottles. I save mine for Mara, who once told me she liked her life on the street. She nods and puts a hand on her shopping cart. "What's your wish?"

"Same as always."

I like Mara. I think we understand one another. We've talked about how, in another era, her ability to scratch out a living from nothing would have been admired, although now people frown upon it. She knows I won't try to talk her into moving to a shelter. I know she doesn't hide the hard truth of her life from me. "We all have choices," she says, and, still, she chooses this.

She raises her hand and draws a star in the air with the grace of a conductor. "Safe travels," she says, and I feel her blessing.

I LEAVE THE PARKING LOT hoping that the hollow feeling in my chest will ease as I put in distance. I want my mind to take flight, but my thoughts keep twisting around the same issue. The two weeks I thought I'd spend here with Josh have turned into six months, in part because the moment we landed I was flattened by a sickness that was hard to diagnose. Josh nursed me back to health, driving me to and from clinics, the lab, and later, the tropical disease specialists in the city. He ousted the guy who had sublet his apartment and set us up there like an established couple. Just the other day, as he placed a cup of coffee in front of me, he said, "We should get your name on the rental agreement and start putting out feelers for jobs, now that you're feeling better."

"Sorry, what?" I held the coffee cup mid-air. "I have a job already."

"Sure, I know, but I thought we could start thinking about the future. These last few months, I've blown through the rest of the money I'd saved to travel. I need to get back to real life. Not that I'm complaining. It's been great. You're great. I couldn't have asked for a better ending to my trip. Cambodia and Laos can wait."

He reached out to take my hand. For a second, I thought he was going to propose. But, instead, he smiled—that Saigon Special smile that had hooked me back in Sapa—and then he licked his lips. "You're the best souvenir I could have brought home. I'll do anything to make you stay."

I have to consciously release my foot on the gas pedal. It's hard to describe how Josh's words make me feel. Tap a slug's tentacles, watch them retract. I know that, in Josh's mind, he's expressing his love, and a part of me wants to be the type of person who would be thrilled and reassured by his message. I know that the chances of meeting another guy as generous and open-hearted are about a million to one. But it's the settling down part that scares the shit out of me, the staying in one place, the loss of independence. I like it out on the road. I love my work. Maybe Josh can't appreciate that because he's never seen me in action—the bursts of grant writing, the meetings with small, passionate NGO boards, the skilled language needed to spur action, prod governments and donors, loosen the flow of money. He can't see that his words cage me in.

I think again of Mara, who once described herself to me as a vagrant, not homeless or any of the other descriptions she might have used. It surprised me, such a particular word, and I think Mara has chosen her own label carefully. Vagrant avoids all the negative connotations of bag lady, bum, or tramp. But it also suggests motion, as if she has no intention of staying in one place.

I'm still trying to figure out how to describe myself. When Josh's sister makes introductions, invariably she says, "Paige flies all around the world doing who knows what. How long have you been doing that, Paige?"

When I answer, eyes turn on me, aghast. Frowns deepen.

"Actually, I'm a freelance writer," I say, trying to explain that my travels are not whimsy, that I'm not taking a long, scenic route to adulthood. I gather data, check facts, find a hook that might goad the advantaged into making a difference for those who need help. "It's activist journalism."

Some of Josh's family and friends are unfiltered. His mom says something about getting it out of my system while I'm still young. His best friend from high school laughs. "Is that what we're calling it now? Wasn't there some girl in town who went off like that after a bad break up?"

They don't mean any harm. They'll loan you their trucks. But I've learned there's a not-so-secret mindset in towns like the ones where Josh and I grew up, a belief that people—especially women—who aren't rooted to a place or attached to a person are somehow unstable. Witness even my father when I told him I was going to stay at Josh's instead of in my old room. "That's good to hear. He's a nice lad. You've been so unsettled all your life."

"You make that sound like a character defect, Dad. Like I'm failing at something. You and Mom were the ones who put maps of the world all over the house. You were the ones touting free spirits."

"Really, Paige, you're not blaming us for that beach birth again, are you?"

AHEAD OF ME, the ocean beckons. Even though it's the rainy season, my aim is to tent on a beach on the wilder, west side of the island. It's a long drive for just one night, but I like highway driving. The journey is as good as the destination. I plug in my phone, pull up a playlist, and force my mind to go blank.

Three hours later, a sign points to my turnoff. The trailhead is a bumpy ride down a rutted logging road just wide enough for one vehicle. Unexpectedly, there are a few trucks in the parking lot. But it's too late to change plans. I heave on my pack and head out, swinging my walking pole, already feeling like I've done the right thing.

The path is easy to follow but not an easy path. It's hilly, muddy, and cross-hatched with roots that grab at the ankles. Water droplets fall from the thick canopy of fir and spruce and find a route between my collar and skin the way only water can. It's ticklish, as if the rainforest has a sense of humour, and I scrape my palm along the bark of a tree as I pass to let the forest know, yeah, I get the joke.

Someone ahead of me has cut faces into bright green leaves with a penknife—faces with expressions of delight, surprise, and fear—and let them flutter to the ground, a crumb trail of shared passage.

I guess I knew this crossroads would come with Josh. The decision to stay or to go. I'd hoped that eventually he might see his way to a different sort of life, but our conversation from last night lingers.

"You can't imagine a life where two people move around the world?" I asked him. "Recording changes, initiating them, seeing the bigger picture? A less traditional life."

"It's got to be hard on their families," he said, pulling me to his side like I needed protection. "And tough for the kids to make friends. You want kids, don't you?"

"Josh, I'm asking you to see past all that. I can't do what I do staying in one place."

When he answered, his tone was hurt. "I think what you're really saying is you can't stay in one place with me."

My walking pole makes a hollow metallic sound as I hit it against a tree on the side of the trail.

THE FRANTIC CALLS of two hikers headed in my direction tell me something's afoot.

"What's up?" I ask, as they slow and catch their breath.

"There's a juvenile orca caught on the rocks. We don't know how it got there—hunting, maybe—but it's stuck until the tide comes in. A few of us have been trying to keep it wet and calm. But we need help, and no one has a phone. We don't have much time."

Already I can feel adrenaline kick in, the wanting to be on the beach helping, problem-solving. There are few enough juvenile orcas in these waters anymore.

"I don't have much with me, but I have a collapsible bucket." There's no point mentioning my phone, still tethered to the truck. There's a pride in being off grid. Until that pride costs.

They're eager to keep going but give me directions. "Head right when you hit the beach. The orca's pretty stressed, but your bucket might help. We're just afraid she'll try to move off the rocks too quickly and injure herself."

They head off at a fast pace, long dark hair bouncing off their backs, and I'm grateful for these local guardians of the sea. I pick up my own pace and hit the sand about thirty minutes later. Right away, I assess the tide. The seaweed left behind when it last receded is still a distance from the waves' froth. The salty smell is more welcoming than any building I've been in.

Down the beach, I see two men standing on a rock bench, a double kayak perched precariously nearby. For a second, I confuse the silhouette of the closest man with Josh, and I hurry forward before I realize that it's impossible; he can't be here.

The men are entirely focused on what's beneath them. One holds a dry bag upturned, emptying the last few drops of water. I scrabble up the rocks to stand next to him and look down.

"Ah, shit," I say, although it's impossible not to be impressed. Not to be awed. The orca's tar-black skin glistens from where it is stuck in a narrow cleft above the lapping water, one fore fin hidden, the dorsal fin and tail flukes scraping against the sharp rock as its massive body heaves. When the creature makes a lung-clearing sound, all I can think of is asthma, COPD, pneumonia. That the struggle to breathe sounds the same for both humanity and nature.

"Right," I say. The orca's skin has dried in an instant. The two young men are tired; I don't know how long they've been hauling this paltry load of water. I drop to my haunches, dump my pack, and begin drawing out my sleeping bag, my tent footprint, my extra clothes. I toss the collapsible bucket to the closer of the men, and he heads back to the water, stretching out his hand to his buddy for the drybag. We are mostly wordless as we work together, taking cues from each other's actions. One fills the bucket and bag and passes them up; one tosses the collected water on the orca below. I inch my way down the rocks making soothing sounds and lay out my sleeping bag and clothes in a way I hope will retain some moisture, protect that precious skin from the air and sun. I sidestep the orca's sightline, as much to avoid making it an eye-to-eye promise as to avoid increasing its stress. Eventually, two other sleeping bags are dropped down next to me, and I lay them out, too.

"Come on, girl. We need you," I murmur, hoping that whatever feistiness got this youth into trouble will get her out of it.

Time passes in grinding repetition. Hours maybe. No matter how many times I scan the ocean for help from offshore, no rescue boats appear. We keep pouring water on the orca, now adding my empty pack and another empty drybag to the rotation. The poor thing has closed its eyes and become still. But the tide is rising.

"Hang in there," says one of the guys, the first time he's spoken. The orca raises its tail fluke up and down as if testing the height of the water, as if echoing my earlier thoughts: should I stay or should I go?

My eyes are on the horizon when it happens. One second, she's there, the next second, she's gone. Success has a flipside I can't avoid. Staring down at the water, at our sleeping bags and clothes churning in the froth, I admit that a decision postponed is not a decision made. I suppose there are ways to find a sense of purpose in the life that Josh is offering. But it's not the same as the exhilaration that comes from pitching in wherever help is needed on a moment's notice. I stare out over the Pacific, wet sand coating the toes of my boots, and scan for the whale or any members of its pod that might be waiting for her. But the ocean's so vast. She could be anywhere by now.

"Did anyone recognize her markings?" I ask. My unused camera is still on the rock where I left it when I first emptied my pack, but a story is spinning into creation in my mind.

"That was the beauty of it," says the man closest to me. "She was definitely a transient, not a resident."

I nod. A transient. And keep nodding.

# Watching Her Breath

The engine shudders and goes silent. The heat inside the car is intense, despite the shade of the pomegranate tree. In the passenger seat, Vanessa sleeps—has slept through flights and meals and the drive from the Bologna airport. Her face looks bruised; blue shadows limn her eyes. She must be hot although there is no perspiration on her skin. When I touch her arm to wake her, it feels like parchment.

Leaving her to sleep, I pull the key out of the ignition and step out into the familiar yard. The house is exactly as I remember: grey stone, red tile roof, emerald-green door. Madonna still leans tipsily in her niche, right palm aloft, fingers missing in a half-handed benediction. Below her, lizards scamper among potted succulents that line the walkway. Enveloped by the scent of lavender, I know without looking that mounds of the mauve blossoms will fill the field below and that the key to the house will be under the clay pot nearest the grape trellis. I hold these thoughts like a shawl and try to merge with the landscape. The bright Mediterranean sunlight makes all the plants look more alive than at home. The sage bush has doubled in size since I was last here, and there are now four rows of lettuce in the garden, not three. At the edge of the lawn, the mullein seems to be competing with the cypress and stands like a soldier, its spikes of yellow blossoms so pollen-laden the bees hover in an ecstatic cloud around it.

Vanessa slips up next to me like a sudden breeze. "It's as beautiful as you said it would be," she says. "I hope it won't make you sad to be back."

We stand together gazing out toward the Adriatic Sea. It glimmers in the distance, framed between two olive trees. My sister is referring to the month I spent here last summer and to the romance that flared between me and Paolo, the farmhouse owner's son. I let the romance fizzle, unable to send my love abroad when it was needed so much at home. So yes, I'm sad, but not so much about the past as about what comes next.

I put an arm around my sister's narrow waist. "I'm glad you like it," I say, ready to steady her as we walk toward the house. "Let me show you inside. You can choose a bedroom and have a rest while I go buy some food."

Vanessa turns her face skyward, eyes closed. "In a minute," she says, and I can almost see her gathering heat and energy from the sunlight on her cheeks. Her smile is beatific, the muscles of her face smooth and relaxed, while mine tighten in a flood of misplaced anger. I want to yell, "Fight, damn you, fight!" But we are well past fighting and no longer able to deny the inevitable. We are only waiting.

THE CORE OF the house is over five hundred years old. Rooms have been added over the centuries, one bedroom two steps down from the kitchen, another five steps up from the sitting room. Settling in takes a long time as Vanessa stops to exclaim over the building's rustic charms. Nothing escapes her notice, not the uneven stone floor tiles, not the cement trough sink, not the saggy velour couch pulled up in front of the fireplace.

"I know it's summer," she says, patting the mantle like an old friend, "but we'll have to have a fire one night." She sounds playful, but the truth is she chills easily, and I promise to haul wood from the shed. She wanders, chooses a bedroom from the four on offer, and keeps wandering. I'm starving for lunch but bite my tongue. "Are you looking for something in particular?" I finally ask.

Again, she flashes me that smile. "No, not really. It's all wonderful. Thank you for bringing me here." She turns completely around like a ballerina on a child's jewellery box, but slower, as if winding down. "I'm just trying to decide where to put my cushion."

FOR HOURS EACH DAY, Vanessa meditates on her cushion. She has terminal cancer: Stage IV, metastasized. Our mother died of the same at forty-two. Vanessa is thirty. I am twenty-seven. Our father died of a heart attack a few years after we lost our mom. We have bad genes.

Vanessa started to meditate soon after her initial diagnosis. I encouraged it since it was better than watching her doubled over sobbing, better than watching her drink herself into a stupor. But a few months ago, I wondered if it was out of control, whether she was spending too much of her remaining life looking inward. "Surely there are things you still want to do," I prompted her. "Surely there are places you still want to see."

"Of course," she said, fluffing her pillow with gentle shakes. "But I can't always be doing or travelling. I have to get through the spaces in between. Meditating helps me find peace there."

I tried to understand what she meant. I even tried to meditate with her. But when I sat, I didn't see on the backs of my eyelids the amorphous peace that Vanessa described. Instead, I saw Italy, its scents and colours and landscape. I wanted to create lasting memories of her against this beautiful backdrop. I didn't want to remember her sitting awkwardly cross-legged, watching her breaths, counting them down.

Two hours later, Vanessa rises from her cushion in the sitting room and joins me in the kitchen where I have been reading and snacking near the window, out of the afternoon sun. The wooden shutters are wide open. The windows of this house have no glass panes or screens. On the marble slab that serves as a table sits a basket of eggs. Vanessa picks one up and cradles it in her palm. This, like so many of her small gestures, makes me gasp a little. I see symbolism in everything.

"Susanna must have left those," I say.

"Susanna?"

"The woman who owns this farmhouse." I've told her this before.

"You mean Paolo's mom?"

"Yes."

"Do you think she's told Paolo you're here?"

"I asked her not to."

"Why?"

I give Vanessa a look that tries to say everything I'm thinking—that this is a time for us to be together, just we sisters, and that I've proved I cannot be happily in love and impossibly sad at the same time.

"Lydia, you can't stop living just because I am," she says quietly.

I lay a simple tray of cheese and bread on the windowsill. "Let's eat outside under the grape arbour," I say.

"You should see him," Vanessa answers, and it strikes me for the first time since she agreed to travel here that I might not be the only sister with an agenda.

THAT NIGHT, I don't sleep; the time change only partly explains it. The house holds memories I did not expect to affect me so deeply. "Look at this kitchen," I remember effusing yesterday to Vanessa, and while she exclaimed over the view from the open window and the colourful pottery, I saw Paolo pouring espresso and smelled the sweet amaretti we dunked in the thick brew. The bedroom we slept in smelled so overpoweringly of his toasty skin that I found myself checking for him behind doors.

I'm cracking eggs for breakfast when Vanessa arrives in the kitchen, swathed in a layered white nightie that makes her look ghostly. She downs pills with cold water while I strike a match to light the gas stove.

"Hungry?" I ask.

"Not really."

She drifts toward her cushion in the sitting room. I'd hoped she'd eat so that we could tour the nearby hill towns, but she is clearly determined to keep her routines. Her morning practice sometimes takes hours.

"Before you start, can I ask something?" I call out. I want to know whether she senses the nearness of her demise. I want to know how much time we have left so that none of it is wasted.

"Uh-huh." From the sound of her voice I can tell she has already started to slip away.

The question is a cruel one anyway, and I'm selfish to want an answer. "It's okay," I say. "Never mind."

I'M ON THE OUTDOOR SWING in my bathing suit when Vanessa's body casts a lancing shadow over mine. She's wearing a sun hat and a cherry-red sundress I've never seen before. She wears it unabashedly, not caring that her ribs and shoulder blades jut through the fabric.

"I've got the map and set the route," she says. "Can you be ready in ten minutes?"

I'm ready in five. The car has a GPS, but Vanessa insists on using the map. "Then I'll be able to say all these wonderful town names out loud," she insists, as she traces her finger along the route and stumbles over all the Italian vowels. "Borgo Massano, Talacchio, Casella. Up ahead, turn right!" It's unnerving to drive in these parts, all unfamiliar roundabouts and narrow roads twisting up and down the hills. Last year, Paolo did all the driving. But I try to match Vanessa's jaunty mood and not show my nervousness.

"So where are we headed?" I ask, although almost any small town would do. They string from east to west, each with its historic fort, each with its cluster of terracotta-coloured houses, its stone laneways too narrow for cars. We are headed toward one of my favourites when Vanessa calls out instructions that take us downhill and onto the agricultural flatlands below. We speed by lush fields and fruit orchards.

"Are we going to the beach?" I ask, surprised.

"No, wait and see," she answers, resting an elbow on the edge of the open passenger-side window, arm floating gently in the airstream. The sunflowers are mesmerizing, and I smile to see her taking them in: row after row of plate-sized yellow blooms, all tilted toward the sun.

Our conversation is sporadic. "Left at the next crossroads," followed by my question about the speed limit. We aren't headed anywhere I recognize.

"See that parking lot on the left?" Vanessa says finally. "That's where we're going."

I'm confused. Ahead, I see a Canadian flag waving across the road. But it's not until we've parked and made our way across the highway that I twig to where we are.

"Seriously? Of all the places we could go, you chose a war memorial?"

Vanessa laughs but says nothing and drifts ahead to put distance between us.

I have to admit, it's strangely compelling: twenty cypresses curving round a high point of land. Tucked behind the trees is a grassy bunker and another semicircular monument of poles angled to the sky to suggest both artillery and an honour guard. Profusions of red geraniums contrast starkly with pale tiling. Here, it says, our Canadian troops broke through the Gothic Line.

Of course, I know why my sister has chosen this place. It is an opening to the conversation we've been avoiding. Despite the loss of our parents, we are not practiced. We need to talk burial or cremation, interment or scattering. We need to talk about how my sister will be memorialized: the music, the flowers, the words on her headstone—all the decisions that will make her impending death real. And we need to talk about whether she will use only pain relief or assistance to get there and my role as her ferryman.

She is waiting, giving me time to inspect the plaques, to prepare. "Fought with valour," I read, and have to dig in my bag for a tissue. When I look up, Vanessa is standing between two spiralling cypresses. In silhouette, she looks newly planted there.

OUR SIXTH DAY IN ITALY and we are both exhausted. If asked, I would say that waiting for the death of a loved one is like running a marathon. The race jars the bones, and the lungs are always constricted.

Today, Vanessa has placed her cushion on the velour couch and leans into its high arms. I think this is because she is letting go now that we've talked; she doesn't feel she has to stay strong anymore. There are other signs that the end is closer at hand: increasing breathlessness and gauntness, a more furrowed brow.

I force myself to watch as she sits. It's a strange quirk of humanity that I'm already imagining what it will be like when she's gone, even while I try to hold fast to every facial expression and file every event we share into my lasting memories. I live with a constant barrage of silent admonishments to *remember this.*

Purposefully I drop the plate I am drying on the stone floor. The shattering china brings Vanessa out of her reverie with a start. I know this must hurt. But I want her with me.

I AM BUILDING A FIRE in the sitting room when there is a knock on the door.

"I'll answer it," says Vanessa, moving with more energy than I've seen in a month. I follow, curious, expecting to see Susanna with more eggs or offerings from the garden.

"Lydia?"

I recognize Paolo's voice and hold back. Did we know each other so little that he is not sure whether he is looking at me? I sense his confusion and can read his thoughts. For a second, he thinks he has discovered the reason I stopped communicating with him.

"I'm so sorry... I didn't mean... I thought..."

My sister swings the door wide open so that I am in view. "Hello, you must be Paolo. I'm Vanessa, Lydia's dying sister. Please come in."

My sister is clever. She knows I will have to rescue poor Paolo from the embarrassment she has caused. He looks at me with both relief and consternation, unsure if he's heard what he thinks he heard.

"I'm sorry I didn't tell you," I say. "My sister has cancer. It's been a rough year." He tries to lock eyes with me but I won't let him.

"Then I should go," he says.

"No," insists Vanessa. "You must come in. Besides, you've brought wine."

"My mother said—"

"Your mother is delightful. I understand from her that you are an amazing cook. Lydia and I haven't eaten yet. Why don't the two of you throw something together? Lydia?"

I have no choice but to nod. Vanessa rubs her hands together like a delighted child. "I'll open the wine," she says, "and leave you two to the cooking."

There is a moment of silence before Paolo rallies. "Gnocchi?" he asks and I repeat, "Gnocchi." We've made the dish together before.

I pull potatoes from the bin under the sink and locate the flour while Paolo puts water on to boil. We work without talking, letting Vanessa fill in the silence between us. She is charming and garrulous, refilling her glass as she tells him the story of her cancer journey like it is a well-rehearsed comedy routine. The wine flush looks good on her.

"I'm telling you all this because I suspect that my sister didn't," she says, stopping to take another gulp of the wine.

For a second, Paolo stops kneading the dough. "No, she didn't."

"So, are you still interested in her?"

"Vanessa, stop!"

"Oh, be quiet please, Lydia. He's here. He came right away. I think we have our answer. Am I right, Paolo?"

I am shaking. "You don't have to say anything," I manage to whisper.

He nudges a fork toward me. Last year, he stood behind me to demonstrate how to roll the small doughballs down the tines, the bare skin of his forearms against mine. It was the first time we touched.

"Just enough pressure so the sauce will cling." I repeat his instructions from that night, knowing he will remember.

"What's that?" My sister leans forward.

But Paolo has heard me and we share a glance.

Vanessa is impatient. "The thing is, Paolo, when you don't have much time, you take care of the things that are important. When my sister was in Italy last year, she and I were in denial about my cancer. But I relapsed while she was away. Now she feels guilty for falling in love with you while I began the real business of dying—"

"Vanessa!" The dough slides off my finger. The fork tines dig into my flesh.

"Sorry, sweetheart, I know this is hard. But I'm taking your advice. I don't want you wasting time grieving. There's a saying about grief anyway—that it's only leftover love." She finishes her wine. "Why don't you two go outside for some sage. When you get back, I'll brown the butter. No rush." Vanessa nods toward her cushion. "You know where to find me."

IT'S A MOONLESS night, for which I am grateful. The scent hits first: the vegetative liveliness of damp grass and the sea air trapped against the hilltops. The sage bush is far enough from the house not to be in the light cast from the windows. I pluck some sprigs, keeping my face in shadow.

"I can't do this, Paolo, I'm sorry. I can't be happy while I'm losing her."

"I don't understand. *Non capisco.*" He cannot translate his confusion, resorts to a thumb-to-fingers gesture with his hands, then a touch to my wrist. "Why did you come back then? It's a gift, *amore*. Your sister gives it to you. To us."

I shake him off. "No, you don't get it. Vanessa is my only family. When she's gone, I'll have no one to fall back on."

"Then let me—how do you say it? Cushion your fall."

I picture Vanessa inside, meditating on a square of fabric and fibrefill that is now worn and flattened. Paolo's choice of words seems significant, and I want to laugh and cry at the same time.

IT'S HAZY. Everything in the yard and on the horizon is a blur. Vanessa sits on the garden swing cocooned in blankets. I imagine her emerging as a butterfly to flit among the lavender.

She sips water from the straw I hold in front of her and draws up her legs so there is space for me to sit. I'm aware of the rough texture of the grass, the hum of flies, the pungent aroma of the leftover cheese on the plate between us. We have said everything that is important to say and sit together in silence. My mind is still restless, but I am getting better at acknowledging and accepting each thought instead of fighting. This is as close to meditation as I can come.

The last few days have been Vanessa's; my nights have been Paolo's. Tomorrow we fly home.

I put the plate on the ground. The crumbs of bread and cheese and the oil attract a colony of ants. They swarm over the white china and their activities look chaotic at first. Ants move forward and back, round and round, over and under the particles of food. When I glance at Vanessa, I see that she is watching as raptly as I am. Over the next four hours, we say nothing to each other, only watch the ants on the plate. Eventually, every scrap of food and every drop of oil has been broken down and removed. There is no obvious system, no single path that the ants use. They bustle about and then, suddenly, they are gone, the plate wiped clean.

From the village, the church bell rings out, even though it is not one of the quarters of the hour. I close my eyes, expecting to feel sore from the long period of inactivity, expecting the nap of the swing cushion to press into my skin and to see the red tinge of anguish on the backs of my eyelids as fear rushes in to consume me again. Instead, I'm aware of my breath, hear it twinned with my sister's. The soft pillow of her palm rests against mine and, in my core, I feel a sense of release.

# Acknowledgements

My LIST OF people to thank runs the risk of being longer than this book.

To my cheerleaders and feedback partners over the years, especially Sara Heinonen, Jennifer Hutchison, Rebecca Upjohn Snyder, Catherine J. Stewart, and the Old Nick gang of Rob Brunet, Scott Mathison, and Kim Murray: my heartfelt thanks. You made my writing better and my life richer. To the many others who have been part of my writing community, thank you for your friendship and generosity.

To the journal editors, submission readers, and jurors who rejected and accepted my stories, you gave me something to aspire to and the encouragement to continue. Huge thanks to the fiction editors of *The Fiddlehead*, *Grain*, *Room Magazine*, *The New Quarterly*, *The Humber Literary Review*, *Agnes and True*, *The Malahat Review*, and *EVENT* for publishing earlier (and sometimes quite different) versions of the stories included here.

To Ryerson University, now Toronto Metropolitan University, thank you for awarding me a Liz Krehm Mentorship, and to my mentor, Susan Glickman, for her close reads, helpful suggestions, and introduction to George Galt.

To George Galt of Stonehewer Books, thank you for the care and attention you gave this book. To Ned Seager, thank you for your thoughtful edits and all the other magic you performed behind the scenes.

To Lynn Thomson, Anne Kennedy, Diana Conconi, and Heather Black, you were there when the only thing that kept me going through challenging times was knowing I had the best of friends. There aren't thanks enough for that.

To my friends and neighbours in Toronto, I miss you all. To my new home, Sidney by the Sea, thanks for welcoming me so warmly.

I won the lottery when it comes to family. To everyone on the Darlington side, the Everard side, and the Valderrama branch, I hope you know how much your love and support mean to me.

To Jim, my partner in life and adventure—on water, snow, ice, and in clouds of mosquitos—I couldn't have done this without you. Let's keep finding places to inspire. And to Gareth, Taylor, and Margarita, your life stories are my favourite stories. Don't ever forget that.

Finally, I can't thank my parents enough. This book is in memory of my father, Robert Arthur Darlington, 1927–2021, who was an author and reader, and led by example.

# About the Author

JANN EVERARD is an award-winning writer whose stories have been published in Canada, the United States, Australia, and New Zealand in journals including *The Malahat Review, The Fiddlehead, The New Quarterly, Prairie Fire, Grain, The Humber Literary Review, EVENT Magazine, Room Magazine,* and *The Dalhousie Review.* Born in Halifax, Jann settled in Toronto, where she worked in health administration and raised two sons. A life-long traveller and outdoorswoman, she now makes her home on Vancouver Island, hiking, kayaking, writing, and being inspired by nature.

# A Note on the Type

*Blue Runaways* is set in Franklin Gothic and Bunyan. Bunyan is a twentieth-century British typeface designed by Eric Gill and digitized in recent years by the Toronto-based foundry Canada Type. Eschewing many of the idiosyncratic design principles on such conspicuous display in Gill's other work, the resulting typeface is readable and unpretentious while still containing a host of charming details suggesting a unique point of view.